Hazel and the Sheriff

DALLAS CONN

authorHOUSE®

AuthorHouse™
1663 Liberty Drive
Bloomington, IN 47403
www.authorhouse.com
Phone: 1 (800) 839-8640

Published by AuthorHouse 02/19/2016

ISBN: 978-1-5049-7939-9 (sc)
ISBN: 978-1-5049-7940-5 (hc)
ISBN: 978-1-5049-7938-2 (e)

Library of Congress Control Number: 2016902558

Print information available on the last page.

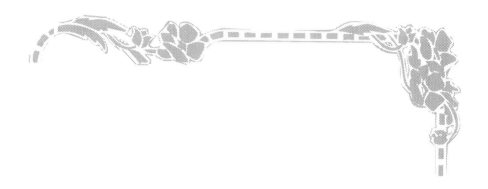

BOOK NUMBER ONE

WHO'S BODY'S IN THE LAKE

Let Hazel tell you this story of murder and the extremes that she and the Sheriff go to, just to solve this case. She will be the one that is telling this story to you and you will find her outspoken and funny. She is a lady from the forties and fifties and that is the time that this crime of murder happens. They go on a wild ride to get their man and how they get them and what they do is why this story is one for the books.

Hazel and the Sheriff like each other but don't always get along well together. They fuss and fight and call each other wild names, just like children but they always pull it together to get their man. Hazel always has to be in control and that's just how she likes it. If anyone doesn't like it and you have what it takes to stand up to Hazel, then by all means go for it. Hazel was raised out in the wild parts of this world and the time period for this story that she is going to tell you is based on the forties and fifties. That's when Hazel was about forty years old.

She has funny sayings and the wit to go along with it. She sure isn't one to push around and she will shoot you if you think that you can stand up to her. She is the best shot in our town and she means business when she tells you that she is going to do something. She will only tell you once and trust me once is more than enough for her.

The Sheriff and Hazel always get who they are going after no matter where they run to hide at. She is not afraid of nothing as you will see. She does have a kind heart but she doesn't always show it. They all live in this little outpost town called Maple Wood. It set just outside of Yellow Stone National Park.

The times for them is hard and they still trust their guns and horses more than they trust their cars and trucks. Hazel is very outspoken and just full of wise cracks. You will love how she tells this story and what she does, with the help of the sheriff to get her man. She shows great love to one family and she is the hope of their town. Set back as she tells you this wild story that starts with "Old Man Jo's first catch of the year."

This story is about trust and the wild trip's that the Sheriff and Hazel go on. You will love the trouble that they cause and the way they handle what comes their way. She will tell you all about it. Everyone that has listened to her tell of this story has loved it and I bet you will also.

CHAPTER ONE

WHOSE BODY'S IN THE LAKE

It was almost spring time and we all could not hardly wait. It had been a frigid and long winter as we were all ready for spring to finally arrive. The days were getting longer and longer, as the sun keep getting higher in the sky. The day was sunny with a few winter clouds still blowing around in the air. All in all, you couldn't ask for a better spring day. The ice in the streams was finally breaking up. You sure could tell that spring was in the air. The birds were flying around looking for places to build their nests this year.

It was a beautiful day at the lake, where we all were enjoying each other and the warm spring day. It had been so cold this winter that we were stuck in our houses almost all winter long. For us to see the winter finally losing it hold on our little town called "Maple Wood," as it made you feel so great inside. We all had cabin fever and most of us was "ready to kill each other", by the time spring finally arrived. All was going great for us, as we were enjoying the first spring day, down by the lake.

That's what we all did every year, for as long as any of us could remember. We got so used to doing it that we treated it like some sort of a holiday. This time was spend, just enjoying each other's company and the arrival of spring. Where we lived was almost at the "Yellow Stone National Forest Reserve". If you are not aware of Yellow Stone, it is a wildlife reserve set aside by "someone in the White House" for wildlife to live on, while living as God had designed them to live. 'Free and wild' 'and without being afraid of fences and cages. There was to be no hunting or fishing there unless you had the right kind of hunting licenses. Yes, you had to buy it from the Forest Department that was set up by our government to get your money. "Face it, they are going to get it somehow, right."

All in all, you had to love living the way that we did or you would never survive the cold winters that we had here. This land was free and wild. Everyone carried a gun of some sorts or another. It was nothing for you to run face to face, with something that didn't care if you were a man or not, it just seen you as dinner most of the time. This was still the most beautiful place in the world. With living here, you had a price to pay. You had to understand that it come with temperatures that would drop down to "fifty degrees below zero." It was still called Gods country by President Hover and, he was right. "It is a site to behold."

We lived in a real small outpost town. "Everyone know everyone, well almost everyone, I should say." This was sometimes a problem, because the chances of them knowing you, means, that they are also known all of your business. People that lived here like to talk about each other as much as they like to eat the first trout that was caught out of the lake every year. We had the biggest fish fry ever spring that you would ever see. That was our way of welcoming, spring's arrival every year.

There was still a lot of ice left over from old man winter's grip, as we called it but you could still find a spot to put your fishing line into the Lake if you looked hard enough for that lucky spot that is. "The spot that had trout in it, of course, is what I meant to say." This year was to turn out to be a little bit different for our small town.

You see while almost all the town's people were enjoying the activities by the lake. There was still some people that had not showed up this year. That in itself was nothing to be alarmed about because we might have been a close and a tiny town, we stilled lived far apart from each other. That's why everyone didn't show up at the same time every year. Money, as well, as time was in short supply around here.

Everything was going great when all of a sudden, old man Jo "yelled out, that he had gotten the first bite of the year. He was happier than a fat groundhog lay out in the sunlight on top of a big rock".

As far as Jo was concerned, the pot of money was already won. We all made a contest out of who would catch the first fish of the year. "Now it didn't have to be the biggest fish, it just had to be a fish." People were betting that they would land the first fish and that would give them, "first bragging rights of the year". They even had a bet on who would win the following year. We did it a little different than most towns did, however. We all bet the year before. It cost you five dollars in the fall, just before the first snowfall of the year. This was what the winner would get, for his winning catch the next spring. This sometimes would run into an enormous sum of money. This year's pot was about "five hundred dollars". That was about a whole years' worth of income for most of the family's that live around here.

They couldn't earn that much money regardless of how hard that they worked. There just was not a whole lot of money to go around, after all. So when you had a chance to make five hundred dollars, just for catching a fishing. "You really got into it." For if you didn't, you had to earn it the hard way. You worked your "brass balls off for it", then you still come up short, most of the times.

Jo let out this "whopper" of a yell when he got the first bite on his line. He was counting the money as he reeled in his line. "Boy it's a big one he yelled out" as his fishing pole was bending almost to the point, which it looked as if it would break before he would be able to land that fish. He was sure excited as he was fighting, the fight of his lifetime.

"The money's all mine he screamed." Everyone else stopped fishing by this time and just watch Jo. After a long struggle, he finally got it close enough to shore to make out what kind of fish that he had caught.

He was fishing out on this big rock by himself, at the edge of the river. The water had to go around that big rock that Jo was fishing on and then the river flowed from there, straight into the lake. Everything that went into the lake had to pass right by where he was fishing at. "James the town's mayor" yelled out to Jo and told him to land that fish before next winner, jokingly." All of a "sudden, Jo stopped screaming and grew silent". We all just stood there watching and wondering what he was doing. He had stopped reeling his fishing pole and was staring straight into the lake water. Something had caught his full attention near the water's edge. "Sam Rogers, was the feed store owner" in town. "Sam, asked Jo," "what was wrong with him?"

Jo didn't answer him. He was just frozen there, just like he was some sort of a statue. Sam walked over, a little closer to where Jo was, just in case he didn't hear him, yelling at him. "Sam asked" Jo, "are you all right?"

Jo looked up from the lake right into Sam's eyes but he didn't say a word, he just continued to stand there, with his "mouth wide open."

"Sam asked," "well Jo, what did you catch?"

Jo said, "well it's not a spring trout, I'm willing to bet you."

"Sam, ask Jo," "how did he know?"

He answered him by saying, it's a body.

"A body," "Sam asked?"

"Yes Sir," Jo said.

"Sam asked him," "was he for real or what?"

Jo replied to Sam and said, "sadly yes."

We all ran over to see if Jo was pulling our leg or not. When we got there, we all had no "doubt" that Jo was being truthful. There at the water's edge was, sure enough, was a body. Jo had hooked it with his fishing rod and pulled it to the lakes edge.

"Who is it Jo," "Sam asked?"

"Hell," Sam said, to Jo, if I knew who it was and I didn't like them, "I would through them back into the lake and let the fish have him." For the life of me Sam, Jo said, I don't know who that is. I was getting some real good bites before this happened, is all that I know. I just don't know Jo said. The fish had done a number on his face and I can't tell who it is with all that damage.

Well, our holiday had officially come to "abrupt stop". Our day of fun in the sun had turned into everyone finding the best fishing spot, into finding the best place to see the body that Jo had found. He had all of our full attention by this time. There is no doubt that Jo had won the bragging rights for this year that much is for sure. He might not have caught the biggest fish but he sure landed the "biggest story of our town".

Dead bodies were nothing unusual for our neck of the woods but you could always tell what had killed them. If it were a great big bear, it would leave nothing behind but blood. As far as a mountain lion goes, it would leave little bits and pieces of it victims up in trees tops. When they had gotten done with the body. They would just simply move to another spot and try again. There was always a lot of tell, tell signs and tracks to follow left behind. That's how you would know what kind of animal, which had killed them.

"For now," "it was all about who was dead in our lake and how did he get there?"

"Was it a man or a woman," we were all wondering and asking each other?"

As I had said before, the wildlife had done a number on the body. It looked as if it had gotten into a "fight with a meat grinder and it had lost that fight". There wasn't too much of the body left over to be identified. The Medical Examiner really had his work cut out for him, with this body. I sure didn't want to be him, about right now.

They thought that the body had been in the water for at least several months. That meant that whoever that body was, had to be in the lake before the waters froze over the last winner. All that we knew was there was a killer out there amongst us.

"The Sheriff said" "that he had been shot with a high-powered Rifle or that's what it, at least, looked like to him."

How he knew that, I don't know but he sure seemed as if he knew what he was really talking about. When someone asked him, how he knew that he was shot.

The Sheriff just said, a fish didn't leave that bigger whole in the back of his head. He would know more when he sent the body off for an autopsy.

"What do we do in the meantime someone asked, the Sheriff?"

The Sheriff said, for us all to go on about our business as if nothing had happened.

Needless to say, our little springtime celebration was for sure, now over with. That body was our business now and finding out which one of us killed him. First the Sheriff would have to know who's that body was.

No one wanted to fish after Jo, caught that body. No matter what the prize was. It was no longer worth five hundred dollars. Even if you was able to catch a fish, Jo still had won the biggest bragging rights, this year. It would be nearly impossible to top what he had pulled into shore, on this day.

Well the body or what was left of it, was being gone over, with a fine tooth comb. They are people all over the shoreline and in the water. They even had a bunch of people out in the lake, in boats.

It was funny because they looked as if they were "duck hunting". They said that they had divers in the water but they sure looked like a bunch of "state workers" looking for a shovel to lean on. You know those people that you always seemed to pass on the side of the highway, with that "look of a deer caught in your headlights of your car, just before they become road kill" or as we would put it. "Diner." I don't know who's paying for all these people's diner, but I sure would like to be a meat whole sealer, about right now.

That didn't stop them, though. They were not leaving a stone unturned. They had all their pitchers were taken and it was time for the remains to be moved to the M.E. office. They just about had to pick the "body up with a pitch fork and shovel's" because it was almost rotted by the time, Jo had hooked it. It was just about rotten, to the point that it was fallen apart. They put it into, this large black bag that would have reminded you, of a large trash bag. They left with the body, to take it to be examined by the pros at the Medical Hospital. That's where the County Morgue was.

It didn't stop there. They were a few strangers left behind to hang yellow taped almost around the whole lake. The tape had some worlds wrote on it that said, "Police tape Active crime scene. Do not cross".

I couldn't help myself, but to ask the Sheriff, who was going to explain the writing, to the wildlife?

The Sheriff just looked at me and he was not looking "amused", with what I had asked him. If looks could kill there would be two bodies on this day, "I reckon".

Well now, all the people had left but the whole town was talking about nothing but Jo's big catch of the day. Let me introduce myself. My name is "Miss Hazel". I run the town's Post Office and Gas station and don't forget the Diner as well. It's all in one big building that has been separated into three parts. From my office, I can see everyone that comes and goes. One of those one stop shopping places. You know what I am talking about. We call it the "Country Mall." What can I say, it a small town.

People around here, just call me nosey Hazel. That nickname, I am very proud of! I will be telling you this story that sat our town apart from all the rest on that day that "Jo caught that body, instead of a Rain Bow Trout."

Now, this is how I work, if there is something worth talking about, I can find out the truth about it or I have been known to add to the tale, "just once and a while." "Who am I kidding, I do that all the time. It is fun and you should try it sometime and you will see for yourself what I am talking about." A lady, such as myself, has to have a little fun now, "doesn't she?"

It's not like there's a whole lot to do around our neck of the woods. You got to stop by my business sometime or another, or just go hungry. Here in my little wrap around store, is where we all hang out and shoot the breeze. "I do mean, talk about each other like dogs but don't tell no one, that I said that of course!"

I get to see everyone that lives in our town at least once a week or so. Everyone has to get gas, food or mail here, just because there is nowhere else to go for over thirty miles in either direction of us, here in Maple Wood. The only other store here just sell hunting supplies and there is a feed store as well as for the hardware store. The feed store belongs to Sam Rogers.

If anyone can find out whose body that was in the lake, it will be the Sheriff and me. His real name is a mystery to us all, here in Maple Wood. He just showed up one day and the old Sheriff had died and he asked for the job so we gave it to him. He only asks us not to ask him what his real name was because he would not ever tell us. That's all. He said that everyone knew him simply as the Sheriff and that name was what he would always be called. "So we all just call him the Sheriff." That's the way he likes it, but if you asked me, it is a pride thing that he has going on.

All I have to do is keep a track of everyone that I see here in our town. If that does not work, all that I have to do is listen to the talk that goes on, here at the store. There is a killer on the loose in our town and I'm going to find out who it is, even if it kills me doing so.

"Was it someone that we all knew," "like a close neighborhood or a friend?"

"Heck," it could be a stranger, which had somehow found their selves in our town and was still hiding out somewhere. Maybe it was a "newbie" that had moved in some were and we just had not seen them, as of yet. You never know, "it could have been one of the wife's that just wanted to swap her man in for a newer model."

The body was the talk of the town. There has not been this much excitement in Maple Wood for as long as I can remember. I'll find out, who that body belongs to first, for I know everything that goes on in our little town. I do sure love a good mystery. They don't say that I have loose lips for nothing unless they don't know me and are looking for a one night stand. Around our parts, you take what you can get. "That's another tell that I will tell you about some other day."

"Around here you never throughout your scraps until you're done sucking on the ham bone! That's what they always said when there was a real good tale, which was going around". All that I have to do is get the rumor mill started. As much as the people were already talking about it, already, I should have that missing person's name, by the end of the week.

There's a killer loose in our town and I going to find who it is. The Sheriff needs all the help that he can get after all because he should have retired a long time ago. He couldn't find a needle in a sewing box because he is so "old and near-sighted." He's all that we got, though. That's because the policeman job came with the only truck that runs worth a crap in our town. It also came with a free gas card from the town people. That's why the man called only the Sheriff, took the job when the last Sheriff died.

CHAPTER TWO

THE TRACK DOWN BEGINS

The Sheriff was eating his usual meal there at my Diner, just like about any other day. He liked to start with two eggs, sunny side up and two slices of country ham on the side. He was shooting the bull crap with the other old timers, at their favorite corner table. I called it the "bragging table." I will tell you all about that some other day. They had just about gotten done with their meal and the tall tales that they were saying to each other when Sadie Mill's came through the front door.

She walked over and took out her Post Office key and opened her locked box to get her mail out. She stood there for a second or two as if there was something really wrong with what she had found in her box. They should have been something there, but what she was looking for, wasn't in the box for her. That was the way that she was looking in her face, as she stood there just staring at her open mailbox. There wasn't nothing in it of course, because I didn't have anything to put into it this morning as I put out the mail. When she stopped staring into that empty box, she raised her head up with tears in her eyes and she saw me looking, right at her.

You don't haft to have a "barn fall on your head" to see that something was very wrong with this picture. She most defiantly had some sort of a problem. There was something, just not right with her as she made her way, over to the bar and grabbed a set. She kept on rubbing her hands together and you could sure tell that she was apprehensive about something, and it had to have been awful. "I walked over to where she was," "to take her order and I asked her," "what she was in the mood for on this beautiful day?"

She hesitated for a moment and said to me, "just coffee." "That's all," "black."

I told her that, I had a mean strawberry pie that was just to die for. "Can I cut you a slice of it, I asked Sadie?"

Sadie "snapped at me" and said if "I wanted a pie, I stayed home and baked one for myself!"

Calm down Miss Sadie, I told her. She sure had her hands full of something that was about to tear her apart from what looked like to me, "from the inside out. She looks as if she had a cat by its tail and she knew that it had sharp teeth on the other end". She had a hold of it and she just couldn't let it go.

"Sadie" "what's wrong dear," "I asked her?"

I put my hand on top of hers, to comfort her a little bit and she was trembling. This girl was shaking for some reason or another. She was scared to death.

"Tell me," "what is it," "that has gotten you so uptight this morning," "I ask Sadie?"

Sadie said that she was sure sorry for snapping at me like that but she had a lot on her mind this morning. I am so sorry for taking it out on you Hazel. You didn't deserve that and I am so sorry for doing that.

I said, to Sadie, don't think no more about it dear. I been snapped at by the best and I am still standing here.

"Tell me what's gotten your panties in such a bind this morning," "Sadie dear, I ask her?"

Sadie said, it's money problems and my husband Bill was the one that spends all of it on Mountain Shine, instead of paying the land taxes for this year, or so that's what, I am afraid he has done with the money, that I gave to him. The money was gone and now he was also. I looked everywhere for him and I still can't find him. No one has even seen him that I have asked this morning.

When the Sheriff got his old hearing aid tuned into what Sadie was saying. He was over there were we were into "shakes of a lamb's tail".

He was right up in Sadie's business and she shut up faster than a "clam looking at a boiling pot of hot water".

"Sadie just stood up when the Sheriff came over to where we were and he asked Sadie," "what was wrong?" When she wouldn't answer him, he asked me, "how much that she owned me, for the coffee?"

I told Sadie, nothing honey, the coffee was on the house. Then she never even bother to answer the Sheriff. Sadie acted as if the Sheriff wasn't even standing there. She just thank me and turned her back to him and walked right out the front door.

The Sheriff stood there watching her leave and then he said, well "I wonder what was up with Sadie this morning." Then he turned and looked at me and he saw that I was not pleased with him at all.

"He just said what!"

"You old fool, I said to him." I would have found out if you had kept your nose out of it. I scolded the Sheriff and told him that he should have kept his big nose out of our business and let me find out what, the real problem was, my own way and not yours. I would have told you eventually. Sometimes, Sheriff, you're too nosy for your sake. You know that I just told you the truth.

"It's my business to know what is going on in these parts, not yours Hazel, the Sheriff told me! The Sheriff snapped out at me. "I have said in the past, so many times, to stay out of it, this time, I really mean it, Hazel, he snapped at me." "Keep your nose out of our business and out of police business, once and for all Hazel, the Sheriff said, with a very sharp tongue!" "Keep your noise to yourself where it belongs, Hazel, the Sheriff, told me!"

The Sheriff said that, I was to stay out of police business, he warned me, "as if". I told him that I would, just as soon as Fred gets back, so we would have a good police officer here in town, to do the job, the right way.

The Sheriff thought for a moment and he said, "Fred" 'with a puzzled look on his face.'

Yes Sheriff "I said Fred," I told him.

Fred has been dead for two years Hazel and you know that.

Yes Sheriff, I do but you were the one that told me that, I was supposed to let the police handle all of this. Well if we are going to get a real police officer to handle this, then we all will have to wait for Fred to rise up from the "grave and do it". He was, after all, the only good police officer that we ever had here in Maple Wood.

The Sheriff put on his hat and he stomped off like a "spoiled child, which was in dire need of the dust being smacked right off his bottom side.

"He had the balls," "to threaten me," "of all people," "like that!" "Who did he, think he was talking to," "Hazel said, out loud."

"What was he thinking by saying that to me," "Hazel said out loud, for everyone to hear?"

After the Sheriff had left, to cool off. I just couldn't get Sadie out of my mind. I needed to find out exactly what was really bothering her so much. I knew that the Sheriff was on his way out there, to Sadie's homestead, to talk to her about her man Bill. That's Sadie's husband name. What the Sheriff doesn't know is that she is a very private person and there was no way that she would open up to him. He'll stick his big foot in his big mouth somehow, I just know it. When he says the first ill word about her man Bill, she will get pissed off at him and tell him absolutely nothing and she would clam up and tell him nothing at all.

Bill might not be much more than a worthless drunk, but he was still the father of Sadie's children. She stilled love him, regardless of his short-comings and she always would. It's not like she was able to find another man, in these parts. Around here a good man was hard to come by. When you was able to find a good man, "you latched yourself to him and you hung on for dear life." I should know what I am talking about, because I have seen them all, coming by the store. They were really not worth writing home to your mother about, that's for sure.

I saddle up my old gray horse and I told Edd the cook, to mind the Diner. I mounted my old gray nag and went the back way to Sadie's place.

Sure enough, Sadie had done exactly what I had said and she had told the Sheriff, absolutely nothing. All that I had to do was watch and wait for him to get shot down, by Sadie and he would leave and I would talk to her, "women to women". The Sheriff stayed for a spell and then

Sadie asked him to leave, just as I thought that she would have. So he left Sadie place, with "his tail tuck between his legs, just like an old dog".

When the cost was clear and, the Sheriff had left. I rode my horse up to where Sadie was hanging out the days wash. I said, my good days to her and she, sure enough, she asked me to get down off of my horse and stay for a spell.

"Sadie asked me," "what was I doing this far out of town?"

I replied and said that I was worried about you ever senses, I saw you this morning, there at the Diner. I just keep making small talk and then, she invited me inside for some coffee and a piece of cake that she had baked, the day before. I was in the door and know all that I had to do, was just to let her talk. That's something that the Sheriff had not done. He's just not that "smart when it comes to women" if you asked me! He asked her, instead of just letting her talk when she was ready to do so. I spend an hour or two just listening to her spill her guts.

She was worried about Bills, aware a bout's. She just knew that he was in some sort of trouble and she was apprehensive about him. He had been gone for almost two weeks, she told me. He had the land tax money with him and she didn't know what he was doing or where he was even at. He was supposed to go straight into town and pay the land taxes and then, he was going to look for work, down by the boat docks.

He said that he would put the receipt from where he had paid the taxes, into our mailbox. When I opened the box and saw that the receipt wasn't there, like it was supposed to be, that's when I knew that, something was badly wrong. I knew how much, that Bill likes to drink, whenever I wasn't around him. He knew how important this was to our family. I thought that I could trust him to do the right thing, this one time. I couldn't help but to think that's, what he had done with the money that I had given to him, to pay the taxes with. I just knew right then, that instead of him paying the taxes, he went and drunk the money up, instead of doing what he should have done with it, to start with. "I should have known better than to trust him with that much money!"

I was unable to get into town, for almost a two weeks after, he had done left home. My sister was coming for a visit and she was going to watch over the children here at our place. She didn't arrive for almost two weeks later than what she was supposed to. That's what made me so late coming into town. I set off for the town as soon as she had arrived.

I know that Bill is not much but he knew how important that, this was to our family. If the taxes are not paid, they will take our land and then, what will we do. "Where will we go," "was what she said," "as she broke down and started to cry?"

If someone found out that he had that much money on him, his life would be in danger.

"I ask Sadie," "how much money, that Bill had on him?"

She said, almost a hundred dollars. That was all that they had. It was enough to pay the tax bill and he should have enough left over to buy some supplies that we needed. When I didn't hear anything from him. I was worried. There was nothing in that mailbox and that's when "I panic there at the Diner". I knew that there was something really wrong, the very second that I open that box and saw that it was empty.

I sat around for a little spell longer and found out what, I needed to know. I said my goodbyes and left with my first clue to who's body that might have been there in the lake. Sadie had not said a word about what had happened the day of the big fish fry. I had to make sure of course. I was up on my horse and I thought of how to find out.

"Sadie did you see the big one that old man Jo caught on Fry-day, there at the lake," "I ask her?"

Sadie told me that, she was not able to attend the festivities this year.

"Sadie ask me," "who won this year's pot of money?"

I told her that Jo had caught the biggest one this year.

"Sadie asked me," "how big was the fish that Jo had caught?"

I told her that I didn't know for sure but it was the biggest one caught that day. I told Sadie that, Jo had won the money pot and the bragging right for this year. She even asked me how much was in the winning pot this year. I told her and then I left her standing in her front door worried about her husband, Bill. I knew then that Sadie didn't know anything about what had actually happened there at the lake, on Fry day.

I knew then and there that Bill had just made his way to the top of my suspect list. Now, of course, he's the first and only one on that list.

I had finally made my way back to town. "Low and behold" there on my front porch of the store building, was the Sheriff. The Sheriff looked at me and said, it is a little late for a beautiful lady like yourself to be out on that old gray mare of yours, isn't it Hazel.

"I ask him," "what are trying to get at Sheriff?"

I do remember asking you, to stay out of police business and leave it up to the professionals.

I would, just as soon as I ever see one of them professional, that you keep talking about.

"Tell me something the Sheriff," "asked Hazel?"

"Were you out visiting with Miss Sadie this afternoon?"

"Yes, Sir," "I was," "Sheriff and so was you and you know it."

"What's it to you anyhow where I go," "I ask the Sheriff?"

"Was I breaking some sort of law by doing the neighbor thing?"

"No Hazel," the Sheriff told me.

"Well," "Sheriff," "I ask him," "what did you find out from Sadie," "when you was out to here place?"

Well, she didn't tell me much and I didn't ask her too much about Bill. I still don't know if that was his body found in the lake or not and Hazel neither do you. So I didn't press the issue much with Sadie. Heck far Hazel, I still don't know if that body is a man's or a women's body.

"Well," then Sheriff, I guess we'll just have to wait for that autopsy to come back, want we Sheriff. "The Sheriff" "asked Hazel," "did Sadie told you anything?"

I said that she told me more than she had told you, Sheriff. Hazel told the Sheriff everything that Sadie had told to her. Both of them agreed that they would have no other choice but to wait for the doctors to get done with what they were doing, with the body's remains before any of them could act on what Sadie had told her. Then they would know more and if Bill Haden showed up in the meantime, they would then start looking for him.

This was not the only time that Bill had not showed up were he said, he was going to be at. If he did get a job with one of the fishing boats, he would be gone for at least two weeks or even longer. That was all up to the vessel's captain, of how long they would stay out fishing before they come back to port. If the fishing were good, it could take a while for them to return to port. There was no way for us to find out until they get back to the docks. Besides Hazel the Sheriff said. I am not too worried about Bill because he likes Moon Shine and as far as I am concerned, he more than likely laid up in some holler, somewhere around here, passed out. He will show up more than likely when one of two things happen. The Moon Shin or the money dries up. Remember Hazel, you said that Sadie had told you that, she had given him a hundred dollars. That much money sure would buy a lot of shine.

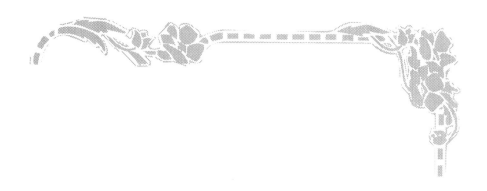

CHAPTER THREE

THE AUTOPSY BACK

The Autopsy had finally gotten back from the Medical Examiner office. The verdict was in and the body that Jo had hooked on Fish Fry day, our holiday. "Was most defiantly a man's body." Hazel and the Sheriff was talking about what the Autopsy had said, as they read it, to each other. The Sheriff had to show the report to Hazel because it came to her first. She was the "Post Master" after all.

The report had said "that it was indeed a man's body but there was a lot of trauma" to it. The Doctor said that someone most defiantly didn't want the body to ever be found. Whoever had done this, had went to great lengths, to make sure that it didn't ever see the light of day again after they, had put the body into the water.

His report read like this. In the doctor's opinion, the body was "unrecognizable". Due to the damage that it had suffered, due to the wildlife and due to the time that the body had spent in the water. He had been shot by a high power rifle. In his opinion it was a "Thirty, Thirty Deer Riffle". It had entered the skull on the left side of the head and blown the whole back right side of his head off. "Death was instantaneously."

There was no point in keeping the body because there was no way to identify who the body was. So the Sheriff and I sent the body to the Morgue so they could bury it. It would be buried in and unmark grave until we found out his real identity.

That's not all, he also wrote that the body had been bound with Bobwire and weighed down with a massive weight, somehow. Such as a "boat Anker" or something that weighed at least, "two hundred pounds", more or less.

The Sheriff and I didn't always see eye to eye but we did work well together. I was well connected and the Sheriff always like to pay attention to the little things, which stuck out at a crime scene. The Sheriff had a way about him to where he could notice all the little things that was out of place. He would always remember, every little thing that he saw at a crime scene. You know like something that was out of place or just didn't belong there to start with. "Well just about every time, we'll leave it at that and move on for now."

The Sheriff, however, didn't have much of a say in telling me everything that he knows. That's because I seemed to know everything before the Sheriff did. He likes to bounce his ideas off me and I was sure to tell him exactly what was on my mind, "whether he like what I had to say or not." He knew that I was a lot of things but he could trust me with his life.

I am, always did what I wanted to and when I wanted to do it. Nobody told me what I could do or not. That would never happen. I was not afraid of man nor beast and everyone knew that about me. I sure didn't care for what people had to say about me. Just so they didn't say it to my face. If they were stupid enough to do that. They got what was coming to them and I would hand them their butts on a silver platter. I would just add to the tall tales, though, "keeping it going on for a while." To me, it was my way to let everyone know, that I was still here "alive and kicking."

I knew that I couldn't tell anything that the autopsy said and the Sheriff was counting on that. For when the real killer was found, only we three would know how the man was actually killed. The Sheriff and the doctor that done the Autopsy and me. The only other person that would know would be the actual killer.

The Sheriff and me and the murderer, as well as the doctor, was all that knew the real truth about whoever that man was, that Jo found in the lake that day. When we found the real killer. Then and only then, would all the pieces of this murder come together. That would be how we would catch him.

All that we had to do was just start a simple little "rumor". "That was my specialty." I was planning on starting a small story about the body and we would just follow the rumor mill from there.

That was a good idea, the Sheriff said. Don't let out nothing that may tip the real killer off Hazel, the Sheriff told me.

"Don't worry Sheriff, this is not my first rodeo, I told him." This is not the first time that I have done this sort of thing. "I conceder myself a pro by now."

The day was going on like so many others had before this one. That's when I decided, to start the tell rolling. I was in the Diner and the Sheriff was back at his usual table. That much would never change. He was sitting with James, the town "Mayor".

That man couldn't "keep a secret if his life depended on it". It wasn't long before he started asking questions about the murder. This man, you sure could set your clock by him and how fast the time that it took him to begin with his noisy questions.

"James" "asked the Sheriff" "if there had been any news on that body that was found at the lake?"

The Sheriff said that there was but he was not sure that he should be talking about it, there in the Diner.

I told him to go ahead Sheriff and tell James about the news of the body being a "man's body. "James asked," "how in the devil," "did the corner know that mess, was, in fact, a man's body?"

The Sheriff told James that all he knew was what the coroner's report said. As for how the corner knew that, he just couldn't tell you but they were still running some more test. You know "Doctors" like to run all types of test James, the Sheriff told him. They will let me know what "drugs and anything else that may be hiding in his blood" later on this week.

The Honorable Mayor was to become their patsy. They knew that he had the "willpower and the work ethic of a snail." He couldn't keep nothing to himself if he tried.

James said that he would not say a word about anything that, they were going to tell him about the case.

They knew right then and there that he was "full of it." Hazel and the Sheriff looked at each other and they knew they had their man, without saying a word to each other. They both knew that they had him hooked. Just like a "big trout, right through the mouth". They would tell him just enough but not too much and then just watch him go.

James was, after all, a full "blooded politician". Everybody knows that you can't trust a politician. Especially if he say's to you, that he would not say a word and then "ads that you can trust him, get real."

"I asked" "the Sheriff" "if they had found out who it was," "that Jo had found?"

As if I didn't "already know the right answer".

The Sheriff answered me and said, that they did but he couldn't tell no one until he made an arrest.

"James" "asked, the Sheriff" "if it was someone that we all knew and trusted to live among use?"

The Sheriff answered him and said, as far as I know, we do.

"Don't we know everybody that lives here?"

The Sheriff answered James question by saying, no sir we don't know everybody that lives here because if we did, we would already know whose body that was that Jo had reeled in at the lake.

After the Sheriff had gotten James full attention. The Sheriff went on with Hazels plan and added that the body had been "tied up somehow." He had dark hair and weighed about two hundred pounds, more or less. That's all that I have to go on, at this time, the "Sheriff said". "Keep all of this to yourself James and don't tell no one. "Not even your wife and children James, the Sheriff told him."

James said that he wouldn't and we sure could count on him to keep this just between us three".

After James had drunk his coffee, "which he was drinking very fast I might add" he said, that he had to go. He had some things to do.

"We know exactly what he was going to do." He was planning on being the first one to tell the news, "Just like we had planned on all along."

"The sad thing was," "James didn't even know that he was being used!"

No sooner did James leave the Diner, Hazel and the Sheriff grabbed a seat right by the front windows there in the Diner.

The store had big picture windows all the way around, the front of the building. You could see all of "Main Street," from where they were sitting at.

James ran up to the very first person that he saw and turned them and his self around, putting their backs towards us so we couldn't see their faces as they were talking.

"Like we didn't already know what they were doing." Just because we couldn't see their faces, that didn't mean that we didn't already know, what they were saying.

You know that I almost felt sorry for the man, "almost I said." This was "almost like going to the races and all we had to do was put the bet down and just set back and watch the pony's run".

We watched James for a while as he made his way up and down Main Street. He run into this person and then that person and they ran into the next person and so on. By the end of the day, everyone that was in town had known, what had happened to the body found at the lake.

They knew what color his hair was and how much he weighed and a few more thing about the body that we didn't even know. We couldn't planned this no better if we tried.

"Let the games begin!"

This was going to be a great way to pass the time the Sheriff said, to Hazel. Now I know why you like doing this sort of thing Hazel the Sheriff told her.

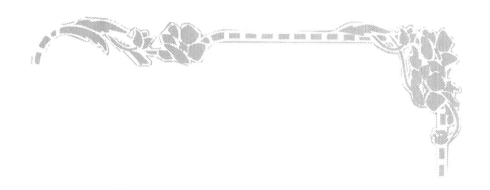

CHAPTER FOUR

A WEEK LATER

There was nothing much that actually happen at least for, the first week or so. Then the Sheriff got a break in the case. Some of our residents here in Maple Wood, live way out into the brush. They just didn't like to be around a lot of people, so they lived out in the bush, all by themselves. That is why we called them "Bush people." They were a whole different breed of people altogether. They didn't come to Maple Wood unless they needed supplies or medical attention.

On this day, the Townson bunch came into town. They always traveled in groups of three or four. How many of them, they're really where was anyone's guess. If they found someone that wanted to live off the beaten path, as they did. They always took them back to the place that they came from, where ever that may have been, at that time. They lived as nomads. First you would see them in one valley and the next time that they were spotted, they could be as many as fifty miles the other direction. They followed the wild game. Where ever the wild game went, so did they. They had to follow the game because that was their only food supply. They had a home base but it was so well hidden, that no one really known, were they actually did live at. That's the way they like it.

They were most defiantly loners and liked their privacy. Some people are just that way. If you asked them a question, they would just answer it, short and to the point. They didn't like to talk to anyone while they were into town. It was if they had, some big secret that they were hiding and they sure didn't want no one to find out what it was. They only talked when they had to and not until then.

What they came for was what they left with. "Nothing more or nothing less." As fast as they blew into town, they blew right back out, just as quickly. Short and sweet and that's the way they liked it. They didn't brother nothing or anyone. Some people just didn't trust them because they didn't do not know anything about them and the way they liked to live. They didn't break no laws by living the way they did so the Sheriff couldn't say nothing to them, even if he wanted to.

This time was different for some reason or another. They stayed just outside the town, down by the lake. They didn't say much to no one but they were fishing for "information." That what first brought them to the Sheriff's and mine attention.

They were really interested in what had happened down by the lake that day for some reason. Every time that they heard someone talking about it in town. They would stop and listen to the town's people as they were talking about what had happened there at the lake. They listen to every word that was said, the day that Jo had found that body. How many of them that was down by the lake, was hard to tell. Every time that you saw them, they seemed, to have someone new with them. "What were they really," "trying to hide" "or even was they trying to hide something to start with?"

That was the question. No one really knows them, so no one really knows anything about them or what they really were doing. They sure stood out like a sore thumb, though. The Sheriff had heard that some of the people was scared to leave their places because they were in town. They didn't know any of them but they didn't trust the first one of them, either.

The Sheriff told me that he was going, to go down to the lake and see if he could find out, what they had in mind to do while they were there, so close to town. He wanted to know why they were sticking around this time because they hadn't done that before. He wanted to know what they were up to. The Sheriff had a lot of questions and now it was time for the Sheriff and myself to find some answers to those questions.

"The Sheriff," "asked me," "if I would like to go fishing with him?"

Naturally, I jumped at the chance to spend some one on one time with the Sheriff. I liked the Sheriff and the Sheriff like me as well but we just never acted on it. They didn't always see eye to eye and both had strong opinions. That keep both of them on their toes all the time. Never letting down their guards. Besides, I knew that the Sheriff was hiding something awful and until I knew what that truly was. I could never tell him my real feelings that I had for him.

"The Sheriff was going to work on the men and I would work, on the women." Together we might find the killer that we both had been looking for.

The Sheriff got a few fishing poles ready for him and Hazel. He didn't want to make them mad, so they were going to act as if they were actually fishing. You don't really know Hazel, the Sheriff said, we might even catch a rainbow trout.

That would actually taste good, I told the Sheriff.

The Townson bunch hadn't done anything wrong, so they couldn't really say anything to them. You can "catch more fly's with honey than you can catch with vinegar the Sheriff told me.

I always caught more flies with horse shit" I told the Sheriff.

You know Sheriff, I am telling you the truth when I said that and you know it.

The sheriff just looked at me and laughed.

We got there at the lake and the Townson bunch had their eyes right on us. They were watching every move that we made and we were watching them as well. You could cut the tension that was in the air, with a knife because it was as thick as we arrived there at the lake where they were at. They sure didn't trust us and you could really tell that.

The Sheriff said hello to them, as we got out our fishing poles. They acted friendly but they stilled moved as if they were trying to hide something. It made all of us feel uneasy, because we didn't trust them and they sure did not trust us, "that much you sure could tell".

I don't blame them but it was hard to get to know someone that refused to talk to you.

We walked over to the spot that Jo had found that body that day and set up some chairs and started to fish. They left us alone for quite a while.

The Sheriff had caught a few fish and I had not even gotten my first bite yet.

The Sheriff laughed at me because he had caught so many fish and I hadn't.

"You old fool," I didn't come out here to fish, I came here to see what we could find out from the Townson bunch and so did you, Sheriff, I told him.

Well, Hazel the Sheriff said to me, if you want to catch some fish, first you have to put some bite on your hook.

I looked at him as if he was the dumpiest man on earth but he was right, I am ashamed to say. I had paid so much attention, to what they were doing, that I had even forgotten to put some bait, onto my hook. I feel like a "real mule's ass" about right now and he was sure rubbing it in.

About the time that I reeled my line in, one of the Townson bunch walked over and said, "Hello to us." He seemed to be a likable fellow. So we struck up a conversation with him and we talked for a little spell. He was over there with us all by his self for some strange reason.

"He was fishing also." But not with a pole but he was just after information from us. He asked the Sheriff all about the body that was found, a few weeks ago.

The Sheriff had told him no more than what he had to. He just repeated what we had told James. Anything else that he had heard was just "icing on the cake" as far as we were concerned.

"The Sheriff" "then asked Mr. Townson," "if he had heard anything other than what the Sheriff had told him?"

He just smiled and stood up just like he was actually leaving us and going back to where the rest of them was at. Then he turned his back towards us but before he got out of hearing range, he said something strange.

"He asked" "if either one of us had been to Jay Cups Hallow lately?"

And with him saying that, he just turned his attention, towards where they were camping at and walked off. He didn't even waited for the Sheriff or me, to reply to what he had asked us.

"Now why would someone like Mr. Townson" "ask us something like that and just leave before the Sheriff and I could answer him?"

He had given use a clue to something that was out there and he wanted us to go there and see for our self. That was our biggest clue yet.

Mr. Townson didn't want no one to hear him, so the Sheriff just looked at me and said, that it is getting late and we best be on our way. So we put all of our things back into the truck and waved goodbye to them as we left the lake.

"They didn't wave back." The man that came over to talk to us, just tipped his hat at us, as we passed him by. They sure are a funny bunch that much we both agreed on. No matter what I thought, they still gave us our best lead and now, all that we had to do was follow up on it. That man knew something that we didn't but he still acted, as if he was scared, to come out and tell us what he knew. We didn't want to push the issue with him, so we just left them all alone. He didn't have to tell us that and we knew it.

We thought up a plan on the way back towards town. It was a long way to Jay Cups Valley from where we were at there in Maple Wood. No roads were leading in or out of there from our town. You had no choice but to travel by horseback, there and back. The hills were so steep and the river cut the whole valley in half. It was after all so far out there that most people had never even seen Jay Cups Valley in their lifetimes.

"The Sheriff" "asked me not to go?"

I looked at him and quickly said, "You are still trying to be funny aren't you. I going and that is that".

He just smiled as if he had a chance in hell, of getting me to stay in town while they went. I might be getting up there in my age Sheriff but as long as I can mount that old gray nag, I can still outride any man in Maple Wood and that does mean for you as well. I told the Sheriff that and he knew that I was telling the whole truth.

He said that I was getting old and that's when, "I reached over and smacked the back of his head, knocking off his big hat.

The windows were down in the truck and his favorite hat flew right out of it and hit the dusty ground behind the truck.

The Sheriff looked back at me and "I knew, he wanted to say something but he was a lot of things but stupid wasn't one of them."

"He just smiled" "and asked me" "why did," "I have to go and do something like that?"

There isn't but one dummy in this truck and it isn't me, I told him. You don't ever tell a lady that she is getting old. You should know better than that. If I wanted to tell you my exact age, I would have told you before now.

The Sheriff stopped the truck and put it in reverse to go back up to where his hat had flew, out the window. When we got back to where his hat went out the window, he stopped the truck and open the door and got out. He looked around for a little bit and never saw his hat.

"The Sheriff asked me if this was the right spot that it fell out of the truck window, isn't it Hazel?"

"I said yes Sheriff," "we were in the right spot."

I ask the Sheriff, was I going to have to get out of this truck and find it for you?

"Just set there in the truck Hazel, said to the Sheriff. Lords knows that you couldn't find a whole in the ground, even if you feel into it face first". Never mind the Sheriff said, to Hazel, I see it down over the hill but there is something else down there with it.

"What do you mean" "Sheriff?"

Something is lying on the ground at the bottom of the hill Hazel but I can't quite make out what it is.

I said, well are you going to go see what it is or do, I have to do everything for you myself.

Stay in the truck, the Sheriff said. I think, I know what it is.

Like I was ever going to listen to what he told me to do.

The Sheriff went on over the hill and there at the very bottom was another body.

I walked over to the other side of the truck where he had gone down, over the hill at.

The Sheriff was looking at the body for a few minutes to learn as much as he could and then he started back up the hill to where I was at. He made it to the top where I was and he didn't say nothing.

I stood there for a second or two and then, "I said" well are you going to tell me who it is, or am I going to have to climb down there and find out for myself, "Sheriff."

Give me a moment to catch my breath, Hazel!

"Catch your breath, I said to him." You couldn't catch a cold you old fool, I told the Sheriff.

After he had gotten his wind back. He told Hazel that the body was Bill, Sadie's man. He two had been shot just like that body that Jo found at the lake. We know have two murders on our hands and we are the only two people in town that can solve them. That has not happened around here for as long as, I can remember. At least by a man's hand, instead of so animals doing it.

"Are you sure" "that he has been murdered" "or did he just fall over the hill drunk and died" "I ask," "the Sheriff?"

Yes, I am sure Hazel because I saw the whole that the gun had made.
I will even bet you, Hazel, that the same gun killed both of them. I will
wait here while you drive the truck back to town and get some help,
out here.

I told the Sheriff that I would.

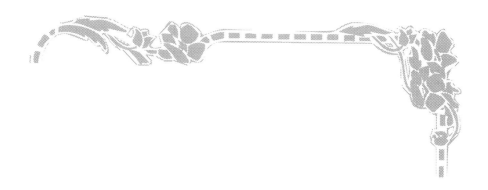

CHAPTER FIVE

NOW THE SECOND BODY IS FOUND

Hazel had made it back to town and got some help for the Sheriff and she sent them out there to where he was at. She was not planning on saying nothing to Sadie about what she knew about Bill untimely death until she talked it over with the Sheriff some more. She would wait for the Sheriff and both of them would ride out to her place and delivered the bad news to Sadie, together.

I have not seen Bill's body but the Sheriff has. I knew there was no way that the Sheriff could be wrong about whose body it really was because he had put Bill in the county drunk tank so many times before.

The Sheriff had the M.E. put Bill's body into a body bag as fast as he could so no one else would see him like that. He told him not to say a word about the shape that Bill body was in, nor did he want him to tell anyone whose body it really was that they had found. We was trying to keep Bill's murder on the down low. The Sheriff didn't want no one to know that it was Bill until he was ready for the news to be told. The M.E. did confirm that he had been shot with the same kind of gun as far as he could tell, there at the scene. He would be more able to tell us more about what had to happen to Bill's body. When he got to do and full examination of the body and he told the Sheriff that he could look more closely at it, in his office.

The Sheriff and I were talking about the other murder the very next day. The Sheriff told me that he just knew that the same gun had been used to kill Bill. He had been doing this job for long enough that he had this feeling deep down inside, that told him, that both murders were related somehow he just didn't know how to prove it yet. There was no shell casing found or spend bullets at either murder seen. The body in the lake could have come from anywhere upstream, the Sheriff said. Where the body was dumped into the water, was up to us to try and find out.

"You talk about a needle in a haystack," I said to the Sheriff. Good luck to you because you'll need a lot of it if you are going to find that needle. As far as Bill's murder scene goes, it was clean. There was not even a footstep to get a boot print from is what the Sheriff told me.

"Who could it have been Sheriff," "I asked him?"

The Sheriff and I both said, at the same time, it must have been a hunter or someone that used a gun a lot. We laughed because we both had said the same thing at the same time and the Sheriff said you know what that means Hazel, "that it had to be someone that we all known." Someone had to know the surrounding area as well as we do, the Sheriff had said.

I said that we had to cross Bill off of our list of suspects and follow the only other lead that we had. That was "Jay Cups Hollower". That was the lead that the Townson bunch had given to us there at the lake. There was something out there that they wanted us to see. We now have no choice but to go to Jay Cups Hollow, where we liked it or not.

From there the first body could have been put into the river, just about anywhere. Jay Cups Hollow was, at least, twenty miles from where we were at in town. There is a lot of hills and valleys between here and there. The first body would have floated downstream from up there somewhere, ending up in the lake where Jo found it. "But that didn't answer" "why Bills body was found so far from the lake!"

"If the lake was to become a dumping ground for murdered body's, then why wasn't Bill's body dump there also?"

"Why didn't they dump Bill's body there in the lake," "instead of dumping it over the hill by the road side" "Hazel asked," "the Sheriff?"

"I" "asked the Sheriff," "was the body tore up like the first one was?"

He said no, it had some animals that had a meal or two out of Bill's body, but that was not what killed him. He did, however, have the same type of head wound that the first body did. That is what made me think that both murders are related to each other. Only the first killer would have known how to kill in the same manner. We have a lot of questions to answer and I say Hazel that it is about time to get some of those answers that we will need to solve these murders. We had to go tell Sadie about Bill's death first and then we will go to Jay Cups Hollow and see what we can dig up there.

The very next day, Hazel and the Sheriff set off out to Sadie's homestead to deliver the bad news about "Bills untimely demise". She took the news about her husband extremely hard. She had three kids and land to pay for. Now she had no choice but to do it by herself.

Bill's passing could not have come at a worse time for Sadie. She told the Sheriff and me that she was with child again. That's all that she needed, was another mouth to feed and now she didn't have no one to help her do that. Bill was now gone and she was in no shape to care for that land and those children all by herself. Sadie was now in real trouble and she needed someone to help her.

I told her to give me a few days and for her and the kids, to move to town, so she could get some help when she needed it. Her place was just too far out of town for anyone to help keep an eye out for them all. Sadie said that she would. Hazel and the Sheriff left her in tears but they had to find the killer and find out why someone was killing people, there in their town.

They made it back to town and started to get some people together for the trip, which they now had to go on. The Sheriff nor I knew, what laid ahead for us but we had to get there and find out why the Townson bunch had told us to go there, to start with. The Sheriff "found four boy's" that he thought that he could trust and we were off.

It was going to take us a week or longer to get to "Jay Cup's Hollower". Neither one of us was looking forwards to that trip. It was going to be "rough as hell" and we all knew it. All that I could think about was how saddle sore that we all were going to be. There were no roads to travel on and you couldn't take a boat because the river was running low this time of the year. The boat motor would drag the bottom of the river bed if we tried to take it, this time of the year. Some places you could walk, right across the river, if you looked for a shallow spot to cross. So horseback was the only other way that we could reach our destination.

We look like we were back in the old, Wild West as we traveled in single file on our horses, around the mountain sides. We moved during the day and camped out at night. We feed ourselves with whatever the boys could find. Wild game was everywhere that you looked. This part of the world was still very wild and untouched by mankind. You couldn't help but to feel free and at peace, with one with nature. This was as close to heaven that you could get, at least that is how I felt. Then my horse tripped and almost fell down the steep mountain side. "That brought me" "back to reality, and fast".

I was the cook for this trip. There isn't a way to cook wild game that I don't know of. Needless to say, we didn't go hungry on this journey. We had traveled for what seemed like forever when we finally made our way up the last hillside to Jay Cups Hollow. It was just on the other side of this last hill.

The Sheriff said for me to stay with the horses, as he took the other four boys with him on foot to see if there was anyone on the other side of the hill. He thought that he had smelled smoke in the air.

I stayed back as he had asked me to do so and they went on ahead. I had come all this way just to "babysit a bunch of old nags". Boy, do I feel right at home I thought to myself. The Sheriff and the boys were gone for at least two hours or more before they had come back to where I was standing with the horses.

"I" "asked the Sheriff," "what if anything did you see on the other side of the hill?"

He said, that there was an old run down cabin, just on the other side of the hill down by the river's edge. There was smoke coming out of the chimney. That means that somebody was home. That's why the Townson bunch had told us to come here to start with. He saw four or five horse in the corral that they had made to hold them. We will have to leave our horses here and travel back to where they are so we can see

50

what they are up to without being heard ourselves. They could just be hunting and fishing there in the river. It might not be the people that we are looking for but I don't want to let them know that we are here, until the time is right.

If we take our horses, they might hear us coming and get the jump on us and I, want to get the jump on them first. We all agreed with the Sheriff, and we tied our horses up and left them there and we set off on foot, as we made our way up the last part of the hillside. There on top of the hill, the Sheriff split us up and he said, that we should surround the cabin from all four sides. He said, to have your guns in your hands but be very sure of your target before you start shooting.

Try not to shoot each other I said, to them as they made their way to all four sides of the cabin. When the shooting starts you will be shooting towards each other, so be sure of your aim before you fire.

The Sheriff waited until we were all in place and then he started to walk up to the front door. The Sheriff had me to stay with him. He wanted me to cover his back as we had gotten closer to the front door of the cabin. They had some dear skins drying out in the sun and what looked like some buffalos hides as well. Both was out of season, so they had already broken the law just by having them there. On the way to the front door, you could smell something that smelled a lot like a bunch of skunks were living nearby.

They were growing weed as well as hunting out of season. The Sheriff sure didn't like drug dealers in our part of the world and he sure didn't like poachers either. Dope plants were everywhere. That was one "cash crop" that was going to be worth a lot of money if they had gotten it to market. They were almost as tall as I was. These boy's sure know how to grow Marijuana. Somebody sure did have a green thumb. The Sheriff was going to put a stop to that, though. These boy's days of growing Marijuana was about to be over with.

Two of the boys, which the Sheriff had brought with us, had stopped and they were filling their pockets full of Marijuana as they made their way towards the cabin. The Sheriff saw what they were doing and he shook his head at them and they knew that they were busted. He was disapproving of what they were doing and he let them know it, by the looks, which he had on his face. So they didn't like it but they emptied out their pockets and got into position.

The Sheriff was going to walk straight up to the front door and try to get the jump on them. Out of nowhere there was a loud noise. One of them had found a "booby trap" that they had set.

"The jig was up." The trap that the drug dealers had set up was full of fishing line that had big fish hooks all over it. Ned was the one that found the big fishing hooks and he just couldn't help but to "scream out as they sunk into his skin, plum to the bone I guess, as loud as he was yelling." All hell broke loose as Ned yelled out in pure agony. The pain that Ned must have been going through sure must have been hell or else he wouldn't screamed out like he did. They sure knew where Ned was at, by now.

They knew then that we were there. Four of them ran out with their guns firing as fast as they could pull the triggers. They were firing their guns at anything that moved. All the Sheriffs' men hit the dirt and the Sheriff ran for cover as they all ran out of the cabin as if their clothes were on fire.

The whole valley was full of the sound of gunfire as, "the fight was on". The Sheriff and his men had hidden and was firing back at the four men. When the Sheriff ran out of bullets he road over onto his back to reload his gun. He look over and saw Hazel, standing straight up like a big target. She was not even trying to hide. Get down women the "Sheriff, yell at Hazel".

You all can lay there in the dirt like fool's I said if you want to but for me, I'm going out with a bang. That is if one of them can hit me before I get them.

Hazel was one to be reckoned with indeed. She was standing there in between those two big pine trees and their bullets were flying right by Hazels head. They were peeling the bark off the trees and cutting the limbs off of them with their bullets, just like they were tree trimmers. The limbs and the tree bark was falling all around Hazel but that only made her fire her gun even faster. She was not scared of nothing, the

Sheriff was thinking to himself as he laid there on his back reloading his pistol.

She, on the other hand, had two pistols on her side and a long range Rifle in her hands. She was giving them as much hell, as they were dishing out. They must have known that they would somehow be caught but they didn't ever think that it would be by a women like Hazel. They had never met anyone like her before and she was introducing herself to them with her guns.

They had never seen a lady like Hazel, before and they would never see one like her again. She was most definitely, one of a kind. They were firing at Hazel and she was firing right back at them. The only differences was she was hitting her target. Hazel, was not trying to kill them but she was attempting to shoot their guns out of their hands.

Hazel, was standing in between two big pine trees as she was firing her gun so fast that it looked more like a flame thrower. She had the barrel of that Riffle so hot that it glowed red.

She finally ran out of bullets and instead of running for cover she through down her Riffle and then she grabbed both of her pistols and went right back to, letting them have it. She never missed a beat as she was unloading her guns right at their heads. She shoots two of their hats right off of their heads. She was putting the fear of God into them, even if she had to use lead to do it with. She was shooting to kill by now and they knew it.

They got a few more shots off in Hazel's direction but they more or less just trimmed the trees that Hazel was standing beside of. I was really impressed by Hazel because she never even moved as they fired upon her. Even as their bullets was cutting through the trees and the limbs and tree bark just keep on falling right down on Hazels head. Anyone else would have run for cover but not Hazel. She was just as suborned with her will power as she was with her bullets.

Finally, they screamed out, we give up. "Call her off they said." I do believe that Hazel had put the fear of God into them. She had got her point across to them and she was not going to move until they were dead or wishing that they were and those boys knew it.

Please, they screamed, call her off before she kills us all. She was, after all, the only one that was left shooting. No one could shoot or reload a gun as fast as Hazel could, but I didn't have to tell them that. She showed them that all by herself.

Something that they didn't know was Hazel had run out of bullets about the same time that they had called her off of them, but they didn't stand a chance after all, against her anyhow. She didn't need our help to get them and they all knew it. "She was a one women show and proud of it."

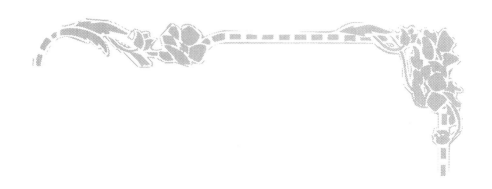

CHAPTER SIX

THE TAKE DOWN

Hazel had saved the day and the bad guys had given up. We all were just fine except for Ned. The fish hooks had tour him up pretty bad but he would survive. We all owed a lot of thanks to Hazel, for the way she had handled all of this. We all helped Hazel, round up the bad guys and they were amazed at the way she had handled the whole thing. She had impressed us all including the bad guys as well. Hazel was a powerhouse to be reckoned with but I already known that and now they all also did. Hazel and I have been through a lot and we are still here to tell about it. Around here that is actually saying something.

I won't forget, what Hazel had done here today and neither will any of us, especially the bad guy. This was one for the books! Hazel and all of the boy's except for Ned, rounded up the bad guys and started asking them some questions. It was funny because every time that I asked them something and they tried to lie. All that I had to do was look towards Hazel.

"All that I" "had to do was" "asked Hazel," "if what they had told, sound right to her or not?"

She would walk a little bit closer towards them and she still had her guns drawn and they would say the truth faster than lighting. They had no clue that her guns were out of bullets.

"I" "asked, them" "if they knew anything about the body that was found in the lake?"

They said yes, as they keep a close eye on Hazels, every move. All that she was doing was walking around them with those empty guns in her hands. She had them in a nerves wreck. One of them said, that Hank Lewis was one of them and that Jimmy had caught him stilling some Marijuana and trying to hide it for himself, so Jimmy killed him because of that very reason. Jimmy had shot him once in the head with his Thirty-Thirty Deer Riffle.

"Now just because they said that they had killed him, didn't necessary mean that they were telling the truth?" The way that Hazel was looking at them, they would have agreed to anything that I had asked.

"The Sheriff," "asked them" "to tell him," "how he was killed?"

He said, that "Jimmy had shot him and killed him with one shot." All that we had to do then was to get rid of his body for Jimmy. We took Hanks body down to the river and threw him in it but his body wouldn't stay down. It kelp coming back up to the top of the water. We knew then that we had to weigh Hanks body down with something heavy. We took some leftover bob wire that we had laying around here and wrapped it around Hanks body. Then we tied the bob wire to one of those blue barrels over there.

"The blue barrels that are over there by your Marijuana plants," "the Sheriff" "asked them?"

Rick was the youngest one of them all. He answered the Sheriff and said yes Sir.

The Sheriff told them that he didn't know too much but those barrels looked like they were made of plastic.

"What do you think Hazel," "the Sheriff asked her?"

"Does that sound like a lie or does that sound like he is telling the truth to me" "Hazel" "the Sheriff asked her?"

"Hazel walked over to where Rick was sitting on the ground with the rest of them. Hazel reached down and grabbed him by his shirt collar and jerked him up off the ground and stood him up to where she could look him straight into his eyes. Hazel had scared him so much that he had wet his pants. She shook him really hard and then she smacked him right across his face busting his lip when she done that.

Let me have this one Sheriff, Hazel said. You can have the other three, I just want this one she said".

The Sheriff just said, "Hazel!"

She said, now Sheriff you know that I like my men young.

"That was all that it took for him to start crying and spilling his guts at the same time." The barrels are full of the potting sole. They are full of the very best potting sole that we could buy to use for our plants. The barrels are massive. That was why we used one of them to way down Hanks body. The handles of the barrels are plastic also and we thought that they would break off as it made its way down the river. They would both find a deep spot and sink right there and never to be seen by no one again.

Why would you put potting soil into those blue barrels to start with the Sheriff asked Rick?

That's how we got the potting sole upstream to where we are now without anyone being the wiser to what we were really doing.

"It worked didn't it Sheriff," "Rick asked?"

Asked me again, after we are done here and then we'll see, the Sheriff side to Rick. Finish your story Rick, the Sheriff told him.

Jimmy would make us take that boat that's tied up over there by the river edge. Down the River, right past Maple Wood and down the river to the next town to where no one knew us. That's where we would buy our supplies that we needed. We knew that if we got that much potting sole from Maple Wood that it would raise some body's attention, to what we were really doing with it. No one would ever buy that much potting sole for their personal use. We used a lot of it on our plants and they sure did grow healthy as you can see for yourselves.

Jimmy yelled at Rick and told him to shut up you fool before you "tell everything and get us hung from the nearest tree."

"Hazel" "walked up right into Jimmy's face and asked the Sheriff" "if she could have that on for target Practice?"

"The Sheriff said to Hazel," "I don't see why not."

Then Jimmy yelled out as Hazel grabbed him by the shirt collar. I tell you the truth Sheriff just call off your "watchdog Jimmy screamed out."

The Sheriff said that he would but if you don't know it by now, Hazel has a mind of her own so if I was you, I start spilling my guts about right know.

All right, all right Jimmy yell at Hazel.

Jimmy promised that he would tell the truth and nothing but the whole truth.

Hazel just looked at him and then, she backhand him right across his face and then she grabbed him by his shirt collar once more.

Jimmy started talking fast and he told them, that the store owner in the next town was on his payroll.

"What about the other body that we found down by the lake roadside" "Hazel," "asked Jimmy?"

"Jimmy just looked at the Hazel with this blank look on his face and then he looked back at Rick.

He was young and very dumb but he was the first one that started to talk.

Hazel let go of Jimmy and she walked back over to where Rick was. "She grabbed him and told him," "that he best get start spilling his guts and, this time, you best not leave out nothing!" "That is if he know what's was good for you".

Rick told them, that "Aaron" was the store owner in the next town and he would sometimes bring us some supplies up to the lake in Maple Wood. We would meet up there and get our stuff and we sometimes pay him some money while we were there. When we were delivering some drugs to him and we were just about done with our business. That's when we heard something moving around in the bushing.

"Well" "what was it, Rick," "Hazel asked?"

"Was it a fat coon or something else," "Hazel" "asked him?"

"No, Rick said, it was just an old drunk.

"Did you kill this old drunk" "Hazel," "asked Rick?"

Rick said, no Miss, Hazel. I told Jimmy and he made Aaron do it. He even told him to make sure that he shoot's him in the head just like Jimmy had shot Hank and nowhere else. Jimmy had even told him to use his Thirty, Thirty Deer Riffle. So Aaron just walked over to him and shoot him in the head, just like Jimmy had shot Hank Lewis.

Aaron knew that if he didn't do what Jimmy had told him to do then, he would kill him too.

Hazel and the Sheriff had solved the case and now all that they had to do was wrap up some loose ends. The Sheriff told two of the boys to burn the Marijuana fields, down to the ground and for one of them to keep a gun on the four prisoners while Hazel and I search the cabin.

The Sheriff told Ned to watch the prisoners. That's because, he was still in a whole lot of pain, because of the fish hooks that was in that booby trap. He was in no shape to do anything else.

When the Sheriff and Hazel, was about to enter the cabin door, The Sheriff stopped and told the two that were burning the Marijuana field, that he would be checking their pockets when they got done with the cabin. They cussed for a little bit but they knew that the Sheriff would check their pockets, just like he said, that he would.

The Sheriff, then told Ned, to make sure that his guns were reloaded with bullets because Hazel guns were out of bullets, even before the shooting had stopped.

The prisoners must have felt like real fools because they really thought that Hazel was going to shoot them if they didn't talk. That would have been hard for her to do that, seeing that she was out of bullets. She had fired her last bullet while they were yelling for us to call her off of them. They had given up on account of no one but her.

They had no way of knowing that. As far as they were concerned she might just as well had a Gatling gun aimed right between their eyes.

The Sheriff and I went on into the cabin and was looking through it for some more evidence. I was about ready to leave when the Sheriff said, waited for a moment. He had found something.

"Hazel" "do you see something wrong with that bottom bunk bed," "the Sheriff" "ask Hazel?"

I looked at the bunk beds for a moment or two and I even went over to where they were and I still didn't see anything wrong.

Sheriff, I think that one of those bullets must have hit you in the head because I don't see anything wrong with them. They are just bunk beds just like you would find in any other cabin like this one.

He said, for me to come over to where he was standing at, so I did as he asked me to do.

He told me to look at the bottom of that lower bunk and tell me what you see. There was sunlight shining through, from the bottom of the bed.

"Why I asked you, Hazel," "would there be light coming from the lower part of that bed?"

"Hell Sheriff," "how would I know," "I told him."

The Sheriff just walked over to where the beds were and reached down and picked up the mattress. The bottom of that bed was lined with wooden planks but the other beds were tied together with rope. Now that is something that you don't see every day Hazel.

"You mean the wood that the bed is laying on Sheriff," "I ask him?"

Yes he said, the rest of the cabin has dirt floors and that bed should be sitting on the ground but yet it's not. Look closely Hazel. The light is coming up through those boards.

"Well" Sheriff, "I be," "this time you are right about something and it's about time!"

The Sheriff walked over and reached down once again and pulled the mattress off the bed altogether. "That's not bedded slats but instead, a trap door Hazel." He grabbed one of the boards and pulled it up.

"Well, I be," "Hazel said!"

There under that bottom bunk was more money than either one of them had ever seen in both of their lifetimes, put together. The Sheriff walked over to the corner of the cabin and there was a feed sack that had some corn in it. He poured it out and brought the feed sack over to Hazel and she started filling it up with the money that they had found.

This must be Jimmy's bed Hazel said, and now it's ours.

The Sheriff said that money is drug money and you know that nothing good could every come from that kind of money.

Hazel thought for a moment and then she thought about something.

The Sheriff told Hazel that he didn't like it when she would get so quite as if she was thinking about something too hard.

I am going to put some of this money to good use, Hazel told the Sheriff.

I have done told you, Hazel, the Sheriff told her, that we can't keep any of that money.

"I said," "that I" "was going to put it to good use not keep it" "you old fool you" Hazel told" "the Sheriff."

The Sheriff was at a loss for words by this time, that's for sure.

I said you just leave it up to me Sheriff. I will take care of everything you wait and see.

The Sheriff knew that he was fighting a losing battle when it comes to fighting with Hazel so he just gives up.

So he just shut up as she walked over to the shelf on the wall by the stove. There was a pretty good size bag of flour. She poured it out on the floor and filled it up with a Hundred Thousand Dollars.

She said you saw how much money that I put into this bag, right Sheriff.

He answered her and said yes mam I did.

Keep this just between us Sheriff and I tell you what we are going to do with this money when we get back to town.

We never said a word to anyone of the rest of the boys and we knew that Jimmy would keep his mouth shut about the money. He was already in enough trouble and he didn't need no more trouble.

It took almost twice as long to get back to town and we were all tired by the time that we had gotten there. But we were not done yet. The case of the two murders was now solved but there was still the matter of the money that we had hidden from all the rest.

After the Sheriff had put the prisoners into jail, he had sent word down the river to the next town and he had the store owner, Aaron arrested for his part in all of this.

I told him to meet me over at the dinner for some supper.

The Sheriff and the boys said they would, as soon as he locked them up and put the horses back into the barn.

I told him not to put the horses up but for him to bring two of them with him over to the dinner. I told him that we had somewhere that we had to go.

He just looked at me really strangely as I walked away from him.

He had gotten done and showed up at the dinner with the boys that we had taken with us. They were back at his favorite table in a matter of moments. "Boy o Boy" if you could only hear some of the tall tales that they were telling about right know. And they say that we women don't know when to shut up. Men just want us to shut up, so we can hear them talk.

I knew that I was not going to get a word in no time soon, so I snuck out of there and got back on my horse, because I had somewhere that I had to be, about right know. I went to see Sadie and I gave her that money that I keep hidden from all the rest of the men but except for the Sheriff. I arrived there and gave the money to Sadie and I lied and said that her husband was killed trying to stop them from killing another person, the night that he got shot.

Sadie said that means that he finally did something with his life besides drink and make babies.

Yes, I told her and for that reason she should get the reward money because of what her husband Bill had done. He died trying to do the right thing, so here is the reward money, Sadie dear. Don't tell no one but the Sheriff I told her. Make sure that you thank him as well. I had that little flour bag tied up so tight and before she could open it, I got up and left. No sooner did I hit the saddle did I hear her yelling and crying with joy in her voice. Sadie was worried when I had arrived and now she would never have to worry about anything every again.

I made it back to the dinner and they didn't even know that I was gone. Boy, I tell you "a lady just can't get no respect at all or least not from them." I feel like a million bucks about right now and that's all that really matters to me.

The Sheriff got up from the table and walked over to where I was and he said, were did you go and I told him that all that he need to know was Sadie and the kids will be just fine. He never said a word, he just smile at me as I smiled back at him. He knew and I knew, that's all that need to know as far as we were involved.

Well, I wonder what the Sheriff and I will get ourselves into tomorrow here in our little town called Maple Wood. "I'll let you know later"! "Love Hazel and the Sheriff!"

BOOK NUMBER TWO

HAZEL AND THE SHERIFF'S RIGHT BACK INTO THE THICK OF IT AGAIN

This story that I am going to tell you is about learning, "that there is more out there if you could only allow yourself to see it." Hazel is a wild woman but she is really smart. Hazel is sure, not afraid of no one or nothing. "She never has backed down from a fight in her life." She helps the Sheriff solve crimes that happens in their little outpost town called Maple Wood. It is a town just on the outskirts of Yellow Stone National Park. She is the one that is going to be telling you this story to you. It is based in the time period O we say the early thirty's may be the in the beginning of the forties. The times here are hard and people use their guns sometimes a little too much. The best way of getting around here is still by horseback.

In this one, the Sheriff and Hazel go to "extremes" to get their man. That's what they always do. But this one will take them far from home and they will have to trust each other more than they had ever before. They get their man no matter where they may run or hide, they still get them. Hazel is very outspoken and mule headed. She doesn't like to be told what to do, that's for sure. Don't try and stand in her way of her getting her man because "she will shoot you". The Sheriff and Hazel don't always get along but they do work great together. The crime of murder and solving the offense can and will take them far from home. You just wait and see for yourself.

This story is about Hazel and the Sheriff and the time period that they live in as much as the crime of murder itself. Back when people still used to shoot and ask questions after the fact. They still trusted their horses more than cars and trucks. It is still early and a very wild time here for everybody.

This story is about Hazel learning how to let her guard down and before she leaves the Indian tribe that she meets, they will teach her so much more about life. She learns the real meaning of life's questions. It is the answers that she finds, that actually opens her eyes wide open to the world that she lives in. Hazel finds herself in love and the way that the Sheriff and her also gets their man is what this tell is all about. The trip that this crime of murder takes them on, just to get their man is what opens all of their eyes. They have some hard choices to make and their will power shall most definitely be tested until it brakes.

The run in with the "Indians and the Mountain Lion", not to say anything about the "Rattlesnake and the wolves" take them on a wild ride. Hazel is the one that will tell this story and you will love her wit and how the sheriff and Hazel work together to solve this crime of murder and suspense. She learns how to open up her mind and heart and what she finds is a "husband" and the difference between "Indians and the White Man." She learns so much about all the different people that she meets and needs just to survive the journey that this case that her and the Sheriff is on.

You will love the way that Hazel and the Sheriff talk and how they work together. Hazel meets the "Sheriff's blood brother" and why he is called "simply the Sheriff." Just set back and let Hazel tell you this story and see if she doesn't impress you as much as she has so many others.

CHAPTER ONE

HAZEL AND THE SHERIFF ARE RIGHT BACK INTO THE THICK OF IT AGAIN!

"Hazel and the Sheriff, was back at the Dinner as usual when Ned came busting through the door's into the Dinner and he told the Sheriff and Hazel that there had been another body found!"

"Hazel" "asked, Ned," "to repeat what he had just said?"

Ned said that there was another body found down by the Lake's, "Camping Ground." He said, "that he seen the body with his own two eyes." I was down there at the lake, down by the water's edge just setting myself up for some night fishing. I was hoping to catch some young catfish so that I could fry them up the next day for supper. I was about to start my campfire so I could make some coffee for myself later on.

That's when I had noticed that, I had forgotten to bring a lighter, so I had no way of starting a fire.

I saw that someone had already had set up their camp site and they had a small fire already going. I thought that they may possibly have an extra lighter that I could use. I went over there to ask them if they had an extra lighter that I could use to light my camp fire with. Whoever that person was, they were already in their sleeping bag. I thought that was a little strange but I didn't think, too much about it. After all, I had no idea who that was or how far that they had travel to get here. There are all kinds of people down there by the lake and I sure don't know all of them.

"Hazel" "told Ned," "if you don't get on with the tale," "I will shot you myself!"

Ned took one look at Hazel and he knew she was really serious, so he finished telling the story. I walked over to where he was laying on the ground in his camping bag.

"I asked him" "if he had a lighter that I could possibly borrow from him?"

He didn't answer me when I asked him the first time.

"So" "I asked him again?"

He still didn't answer me back. I walked over to him and I stuck my hand down to where he was laying and I shook him a little bit, just a little bit Sheriff mind you but he still didn't move. He just laid there, so I shook him just a little bit harder and he still didn't move. "I knew then that something was wrong with him." I pulled the camping bag off of his head and then I asked, him to wake up. He still didn't move.

"Hazel said," "Ned," "get on with it or do you think I am really kidding you when I told you that I would shoot you?"

No, Ned said, Miss Hazel. I pulled the camping bag down a little bit more and that's when I felt something wet on my hands. I look at my hands and they were covered in blood Sheriff, Ned said. It was "blood Sheriff", "Ned said." "It was blood!"

I heard you the first time the Sheriff told Ned.

Ned just keeps on repeating himself, over and over again because his nerves were torn up by what had happened to him.

I heard you the first time that you said it, Ned, the Sheriff told him.

I took off running and jumped on my horse and came straight here, to tell you, Sheriff.

The Sheriff said that he would take care of it. Ned, you go back to where you found the body and make sure no one touches anything.

"Ned turned and started out the door when the Sheriff asked him" "to come back here for a second?"

I don't want anyone to touch that body and Ned that means you too. Leave everything just the way you found it Ned until Hazel and I get out there.

"You do understand what I said, didn't you Ned," "the Sheriff ask him again?"

Ned said yes he understood everything that he told him. I won't, Ned said to the Sheriff, I will do just as you told me to do. You can count on me Ned said, to the Sheriff and then he left to go back out there to the lake.

The Sheriff and I, work on all types of crime, which happens around here in Maple Wood. From murder to whatever. The "Sheriff's real name is Sheriff". I know that that's sounds funny but he doesn't like anyone to know his first nor his last name. It's a pride thing for him, that's all. It's just about like me, I don't want no one to know my last name. That's just because it's really isn't anybody's business. For as far as I am concerned, people can get to be too noisy, if you let them that is.

This place was set aside for the wildlife to remain wild and free forever. Our town is what you might call an outpost town. It is, in all, a really quiet place to raise your family. The Sheriff and I don't always see things "eye to eye" but we do however work well together, most of the time. We are both strong-minded and very opinionated of each other, but we are great friends. Somehow we manage to always put it together and get our man".

"As for this last murder goes all that I have to say is, here we go again!"

The Sheriff had rounded up some of the boys to help with whatever that we would find, down by the campground where Ned said, that he found the latest body at. There was "Fredrick, Sam, Jo, and Will."

Fred was short for Fredrick" so that was what we all called him. His "father was Fred", he was the last Sheriff, that we had here in Maple Wood. He "died" a while back and that's when the Sheriff that we have now, took over for him. He has been here every sense.

No one really knows what the Sheriff's real name is and that the way he likes it. The Sheriff had jumped right into the thick of it and called for the Medical Examiner or sometimes just called "M.E" for him to get his team together and for them all to meet us down by the lake, at the camping grounds where Ned had found the body at.

We all had arrived at the camping grounds by the lake and they were all over the place doing their jobs. They were good at what they done. They took great pride in their work. They were taking pitchers and some of them were taking soil samples as well. They took everything including the tent and what was left of the campfire.

The Sheriff and I were looking at the body and the place that it was laying for anything, that might stick out, that would tell us something about what had happened here. He looked so peaceful and as if he was just lying there on the ground sleeping. There was not even any sign of a struggle or a fight. We couldn't find anything, there but his body laying at on the ground.

The M.E said that he had been stabbed twice and that was what had killed him. Once in the groin and the second time, in the chest. That one was the fatal strike. It had pierced his heart. He had bled out in just seconds.

Notice his mouth, see the redness around his lips and nose, which will turn into a bruise, later on, that's because someone had held his nose and mouth closed. Whoever did this to him come up from behind him and he didn't stand a chance after that. I would say that happen because they didn't want him to yell out and draw any unnecessary attention to what they were doing. That's why he was killed here and so many people were around but yet no one heard or saw nothing.

With us not being able to find anything where the body was to help us, we expanded our search around the whole campgrounds. The Sheriff and I were walking around to all the camping sites that didn't have anybody staying at them. The Sheriff was checking the fire pits out as we went to see if any of them were still hot.

We had searched all of them and the last one was still warm. The Sheriff stood up from where the fire pit was and it was a straight shot from where he was standing to where the body was found. This is where the killer was camping at the Sheriff said. From here he had a clear shot to the other camping site where the body was found.

Go back around the campsite and asked if anyone noticed anything about who might have stayed here last night. One of the other campers said that they had indeed seen some young man that was staying there. He was camping by his self. He had been here for at least three days that I know of because my family had been here all week. He was about twenty or twenty-five years old or that's how old he had looked to me, anyhow. There was something funny about the way he was handling himself. That is what made me pay close attention to him. "The Sheriff" "asked the man," "what he meant by saying that?"

He said that every time that someone got to close, to where he was, he would just go inside of his tent and he would even zip the door close. As far as I know Sheriff, I never saw him talking to anyone here at the campgrounds. We all left him alone because we thought that he might have been a homeless person or there was just something really wrong with his head. You know what I am saying. We thought that he might be a "little bit off of his rocker." He was gone before we knew it. One of them said that they saw him leaving and he went towards the park.

"You mean he left in the direction of Yellow Stone" "Hazel asked?"

The man said, yes Hazel that was the way that he had gone.

"How long ago was that" "the Sheriff asked," "the man?"

He said that it was about four or five hours ago. The Sheriff thanked everyone for their help and we went back to the Diner to plan out our strategy.

The Sheriff and I were sitting there at his table and he asked me.

"When was the last time that she had seen anyone from the Indians tribes?"

Hazel looked at him and she said, you know Sheriff that they never come to town except in the fall. That's when they do their trading every year.

"Now why," "would you ask me," such a thing like that to start with Sheriff," "Hazel ask him?"

The Sheriff said, that he had some friends in low places and that we needed their help to solve this one Hazel.

I was very confused, with what he had just said, to me.

Sheriff, I do believe that you have lost what little mind that you have left!

Hazel the Sheriff said, I mean that we are going on a trip to the Indian camp.

"Why should we go all the way out there where they live at?"

The Sheriff told Hazel that he had to talk to the chief.

"I ask," "the Sheriff," "do you have any idea how far the Indians tribe is from here?"

The Sheriff said, yes Hazel I do. It is about a week's journey from here and we will need their help in this case. We will need to track that fellow down and there at the Indian tribe, they have the best trackers in our neck of woods. We're going to need his help to find this man if we plan on finding him at all. Where he has run off to, he could go just about go anywhere there in Yellow Stone Park that he wants to go. He could be lost to us forever but not to the Indian trackers. They can find him no matter where he runs to hide at.

We will get the horses ready for the trip and we will need to take all of our supplies with us, as we go. We can't hunt off the land in Yellow Stone. We will also need to take a pack Mule with us to carry everything. We will all so need to take some Tobacco with us as well as for some Whisky. Get the best Whisky that you have got in stock.

I said, what!

The Sheriff told Hazel that if you want to do business with the Blackfoot Indians, you must first wet their Whistles with Whisky and they like to smoke white man's Tobacco.

Hazel never asked him any more questions but instead, she just started getting everything that the Sheriff had asked for ready, for the trip that they would be taken the next day.

By the next day, we had all of our supplies ready and packed up on the mules backpack and we were on our way to the Indian tribe. They were a tribe of Indians that lived as far back in one of the deepest valleys that were around Yellow Stone Park. That was their destination. They lived so far back in that valley, which unless you were looking for them you would never know that they were back there.

You could always count on them to watch your every move that you made, though. They always keep an eye on anyone that got to close to where they tribe was but you would never see them until they wanted you to.

They were called the Blackfoot Indian tribe. They were different tribes and they all had their own ways of living. They were friendly as long, as you were nice to them and always showed them respect. You had to obey their ways and their tradition. If you were stupid enough to cross them. We'll just say that you would never be seen again. They didn't play around with outsiders. They lived so far off the beaten path that you couldn't find help, even if you tried.

There they were the law and they handed out their own kind of justice when they needed to. No judge or jury there, they just shot you or skin you alive. It was all about how mad that you had gotten them. That's one hornets nest that you didn't want to shake a stick at. Trust me when I tell you that.

We were now leaving our world and interring into theirs. The trip was going to be long and hard but I was in good company and that somehow made it a little bit easier. I am of course referring to the Jackass and not the Sheriff, but don't tell him that I said that.

This place always seemed to take my breath away. Everywhere that you looked, you could always see something different. We were just strolling along enjoying all the beautiful views. I could do this forever.

"There was places that we had to pass by such as the Minty Grand Canyons and the Geyser called Old Faithful."

"Did you know that it erupted every ninety-one minutes on the dot!?"

There was also huge open meadows. They seemed to go on forever and ever. You could see some of the wildlife, such as for the Wolfs and the Black Bears. There was also Elk and Deer and the Subalpine Forest. This place really had it all.

"If this is not what heaven looks like," "I don't think that I want to go anywhere else?"

The one part that I didn't like was the Earth Quakes. "Yes," "I said," "Earth Quakes!"

Yellow stone experiences thousands of them every year. Some are small but some of them "really scare the dickens out of you!"

The clouds were what the Sheriff said, that we were following. As long as we follow them we won't get lost he said.

"I said" "the clouds!"

He said, yes and he pointed up to the sky.

"Do you see those clouds that seemed to go on forever Hazel" "he asks me?"

"I said," "yes" "what about them" "I asked him?"

He said that they are called Pyrocumulus Clouds.

"Can you see the direction that they are going in?"

"Yes," I told him.

That is the direction that we have to go, the Sheriff said. We will use them like they were a road map. When they go over the highest mountain, we will almost be there. That's when we should see some sort of a sign, of the Blackfoot tribe. Don't worry they will find us first.

"I wasn't worried until you said that," "I told him!"

I plan on them finding us, the Sheriff said, because if they don't, we could never find them.

"How do you know, that who we are looking for, has even come this way?"

I know because I have been tracking him sense we left town. He must have had a horse or he stolen one because we are following his horse tracks. The good news is that he is alone. Unless he is planning on meeting up with someone else out here, we should be just fine and if he does, we will do what we always did. Handle one problem at a time Hazel.

All that I know Hazel said, to the Sheriff, I hope that you best know where we are going.

He said just set back in the saddle and enjoy the ride, Hazel.

"I told him" "that I would if my behind didn't feel like I was sitting on top of a cactus about right now!" Hazel said that she was sore in places that a lady such as for herself should never be.

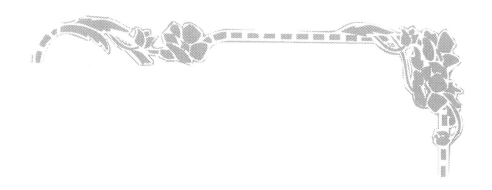

CHAPTER TWO

HAZEL THE SHERIFF AND
THE MOUNTAIN LION

Hazel and the Sheriff had been on the trail for almost a full week now. They were so tired by this time and there was a Mountain Lion that keep the horses spoke almost, all of last night. They didn't get much sleep on account of that Lion. The Lion had to be close by because you could tell, by how fast the horses was moving their ears. We keep the horses feet hobbled at night, so they would not run off in the dark of night. They would sure find nothing out there but death.

When I said that we keep the horses feet hobbled, what that means is when you tie one front foot of the horse's leg to the other one. That way they can be left loose to graze on the grass but they can't get too far away. They are unable to run because their legs are tied together. They would naturally just fall down if they even tried to run. They had to hop along as they picked the grass. The Sheriff stayed up with them on Guard all night and he told me to get some sleep while he keep watch on the horses. I laid down but I didn't sleep any, the whole night long. He was guarding the horses and I was guarding him.

"Mountain lions are nothing to sneeze at. They would rip you to shreds in a matter of seconds and the horse knew that too. Their diets commonly were made up from Deer and Elk, Mice and they would also take down a small Buffalo Calf.

If your horses got free in the middle of the night. The first thing that you would want to do was run after them so they wouldn't get away from you. That's not a good idea. It was best to wait until the next morning then track them down, because they were some things out there, in the dark that would most defiantly bite you back. You had to be on Guard for Rattlesnakes as well as for Robbers, not to say anything about Mountain Lions.

There was also some good Indians as well as for bad ones. "You could say the same thing about the White Man as well," They were called Rogue Indians. That meant that they didn't have a home of their own. They lived off of whatever came their way. They were cast out of their tribes most of the time because they wanted to do what they wanted to do, instead of following their chief's rules. They are very dangerous indeed. They don't live by nobody's rules. They are pretty much did as they pleased.

"Mountains Lions was more dangerous when they were protecting their kill that they had made or when you got to close to their den. You sure didn't want to run onto one when she had her young with her either. They would come at you and yes they would have only one thing on their mind. That would be to take the threat out. Even if it cost them their own lives. "They would fight to kill for their young."

"So you see that's why the Sheriff is watching the horses so carefully. He can't hear the Lions as good as the horses can smell them". There was, however, some ways to protect yourself. By chance, if you ran up on a Lion. You should always keep and maintain eye contact and whatever you do don't turn away, not even for a second. Stand up straight and put your arms out to your sides. You want to look as big, as you could possibly be. Try to make him think that you are to larger prey for him to take down. In case, the Lion is guarding her den and you walked up on it without realizing what you have done, until it's too late. Back away from that spot and never, ever try to outrun one. "You can't."

"When you run you look more like prey to them and they will most defiantly, chase after you. If the Lion comes towards you, it is trying to get you to run, but don't. Stand your ground and find something that you could use as a weapon. Like rocks and even tree branches and if all else fails, fight for your life and fight hard because that Lion sure will be, that you can bank on."

The next day we had gotten everything ready and we were off. There was this big open meadow that we had no choice but to cross. The field was full of tall grasses and there were a lot of places, which anything could be hiding at, just waiting to launch an attack. We could be ambushed just about anywhere, at any time. It might have looked as beautiful as the winds blew through the tall grass but out here, you always had to stay on guard, at all times.

The horses still had their ears up and they were watching every step that they were making. Know this is scary indeed. You just couldn't see anything and that's, what made you feel so uneasy. Finally, we made it through the high grass and we all were feeling, such relief when we had made it, though.

I told the Sheriff that I was feeling better now that we were out of there.

He said that was scary but I didn't dread that near as much as I dread, what we still have to go, though.

"I asked him," "what he meant by saying that?"

He said that we are getting ready to go through the Grouch. That is when we will have to keep a close eye out, so we don't get ambushed by something. The hills and the steep cliffs would make a great hiding place for just about anything. We could finally find that Lion that had been following us for some time now.

That is one thing that I don't want to find, that's for sure I told him.

The Sheriff said that it would be better for us if we found it before it could ambush us up ahead somewhere. Hazel, you go on in front and I bring up the rear. If anything decides to attacks us. It will attack the rear first.

The pass that we had to go through was just wide enough for one of us at a time to go through. The cliffs were so steep and the brush was very thick but that was the only way that we had to go. I was scared but I knew that I had to do it, so I did.

We were just about threw the pass when out of nowhere, "that Mountain Lion decided, that was a good place to attack us." He had done just as the Sheriff had said it would have. He was in the rear and that was where he struck. The Sheriff had been leading the pack mule behind of him and the Lion went for the pack mule first.

"He jumped off of a high cliff and landed right on the back of that Mule while sinking his razor sharp claws into its hide. The deeper the Lion sunk its claws, the more that the Mule bucked." The Mule took off running right past the Sheriff. He was trying to get that Lion off of the Mules back. This in return caused the other horses to start bucking and going crazy. "All hell had broken lose." They must have thought that the Lion was on their backs also.

"The Lion let out this extremely loud Squall that sent chills down my spine!" I couldn't help the Sheriff because my horse was going wild right along with the rest of them. I was having a time controlling him.

"When I regained control of my horse, I turned back around just in time to see the Sheriff diving off of his horse and onto the back of that Lion, which still had his claws sunk into the Mules back. The Lion let go of the Mule and the Mule took off running right past me. He was out of there."

I made my horse run up to where the Lion and the Sheriff both had tumbled down over the hill at. I couldn't see them but they were sure cutting a fit. The noise that they were both making just echoes throughout the entire valley that we were in. I jumped off my horse and ran down the steep hillside, towards where I thought that they were. I slipped and fell all the way to the bottom.

There was the Lion and the Sheriff. He had hold of the Lion and the Lion had hold of him. They were rolling around fighting on the ground in front of me. I had my gun in my hand and I was waiting for a clear shot but I didn't take it because I was too afraid of shooting the Sheriff instead of the Lion. This went on for what seemed like forever. I couldn't tell who was winning. They were kicking up too much dust for me to see too much.

Then the Lion let out this big Squall, just like it had done when it attacked the Mule and the fight was over. There they both laid in front of me on top of each other. Neither one of them was moving by this time. I just knew that my best friend had just lost his life while he was protecting that old Mule and me.

I walked over to where they both were laying there on the ground at and I shook the Lion with my foot to see if it was dead or alive. It didn't move and I saw that it was dead. The Sheriff had stabbed it to death with his hunting knife. Then the Sheriff, who I thought was just as dead as the Lion was moved a little bit. I was so relieved.

"He said," "well women are you just going to stand there or are you going to get this thing off of the top of me?"

"I was so relieved to hearing him, bark out orders at me!" He would have never gotten by with that any other time but this time, I will let it go.

I reached down and pulled the Lion's dead body off of him. The first thing that I saw was a whole lot of blood.

The Sheriff said that it not as bad as it looks Hazel, he said.

I told him takes because you are not looking at it from my point of view.

The Lion had torn him up pretty bad. He just didn't know it, at this time.

I said, you feel that in the morning.

Hell women I feel it right know, he said. I don't have to wait for the morning. He said that he was getting too old for this and then he just closed his eyes.

I thought that he had done went and died on me right then and there.

I always was one that liked to be in control but this time, I was so lost. I didn't know what to do. I thought for a moment and then I said, to myself that, I had to snap out of it. I had to take charge and stop being in control of my life and take charge of this right now. I was now the only one that we both had to depend on. I bent down and checked to see if he was dead or alive. To my relief, he was still breathing.

"Now" "what," "I asked myself?"

I looked around to see what that I had to work with. I knew that I had to get the bleeding to stop before he bleeds out. We were on a level spot just above the river, which was a good thing I thought to myself. I had water and I knew that I could find food.

I started out by looking after the Sheriff like he had done for me, so many times before. I took his hat and used it to go down to the river's edge, to get some water so that I could clean and dress his wounds. He was torn up pretty bad. I took off his clothes and built a fire for heat. I needed to dress his wounds with warm water. Out here infection would kill you faster than lighting but not before it made you suffer first. I checked his injuries and he had some deep cuts that would need stitching up. I was going to have to sew him up and I knew how to do it.

After I made sure that he was as comfortable as I could possibly make him. I went and rounded up the horses. The Mule was cut up bad but he would make it all right. He couldn't carry anything but I thought that if I needed him to, at least, he could drag the Sheriff out of here. He would be at least able to do that much or at least, I hoped that he could. I gather up some long poles and I made a sheltered for the Sheriff and myself.

I had no idea where we were at and I just couldn't worry about that right now. I went back to dressing the Sheriff's wounds and I took some long hairs from the mule's tail and sew up his deepest cuts.

Mule's tail hairs are very strong and course. They were all that I had to stitch him up with and that was what I used. I had took care of him the best that I could have and I went down to the riverside and caught some fish. I cook them by the fire and fed them to the Sheriff. He was not moving and I was really worried about him.

"How was I going to get him out of here I keep thinking to myself?"

I was in the middle of nowhere and I now had to drag him everywhere that we went. I come up with a plan and set out to put it into motion. I would stay here for at least the next few days and if he got better great but if there was no change in him by that time. I was going to have to find help somehow. It has been almost a week now and the Sheriff still had not woken up. He just laid there motionless so still and calm. I really didn't think that he was going to make it.

I was not willing to give up on him yet. He had started to heal all except for, one place on his leg. The cat had ripped his flesh to the bone. Regardless of what I had already done, he had set up an infection in his leg and he was now running a high fever. That is the first sign of Gain Green. If he took that, he would surely die.

If I didn't act fast, I was sure to lose him. The infection was deep and it was starting to spread very rapidly by this time. I knew that they were only two things that I could possibly do by now, to save his life. I was not about to let him die while on my watch. That was to remove his leg with the infection in it and try to save his life that way or burn it out. Either one was going to change his life forever.

I built the fire up and got it as hot as I could. There was a big metal spoon that I had brought with us, so I put it into the red hot ashes of the fire. I cleaned his wound as good as I could. I told him what I was going to do. I wasn't sure that he could hear me but I told him anyhow, it just made me feel better.

I reached over and got that big spoon by the handle with some cloth that I had wrapped around my hand to keep the spoon from burning me. I took a deep breath and told him that I was so sorry for what I have to do but it has to be done. "The spoon was glowing red because the fire was so hot." "I sat down on top of his leg and I shoved that red hot soon, down into his cut. I shoved that spoon as deep and as far, as I possibly could."

"The smoke and the smell of burning flesh was almost more than I could stand." The Sheriff let out the loudest scream that I had ever heard in my lifetime and then he got as stiff as a board for a moment or two and then he went back limp! I had either killed him or saved him by what I had done. I threw that spoon so hard that it went plum across the river. I was in tears myself as I could do nothing else but lay down beside of my best friend. I stayed there beside him for the rest of the night.

The next morning had come and I was awakened by him putting his arm around me.

He said something to me that for as long as I live, I will never forget.

He said there, there old women, it's all going to be just fine. He was worried about me instead of himself.

I hugged him so hard that it must have hurt him because he moaned but I didn't really care at this moment in time. I knew then and there that he was going to be just fine!

'We just laid there on that hard ground in each other's arms for the rest of that night. I was wrong when I told you that, Yellow Stone Park was the closest that you could get to Heaven, this was!'

I took care of him for the next couple hours when I heard something coming down the pathway towards us. Whoever it was they were on horseback. I thought that it could be a Mountain Man or, at least, someone that could help us, get out of here. Then everything suddenly grew so quite. I didn't see no one or hear no one anymore.

"Where did they go," "I thought to myself?"

I turned over and put my back towards the Sheriff. I had my gun drowned and I sure wasn't afraid to use it. Then out of nowhere there was Indians, all the way around us. I just knew that we were both dead. I had no idea if they were friendly or if they were Rogue Indians.

They had jumped us from behind just as I was about to shoot. The little stick shelter that I had made for the Sheriff and for myself was no match for those Indians. They knew exactly what they were doing. When they had my gun out of my hand, there was a really big Indian that was walking over to where we were. I told him that we had run into a Mountain Lion and I was doctoring my friend's wounds. I told him that we meant them no harm.

He said something to the others in their own tongue and he walked closer to us and he pushed me away from the Sheriff.

I couldn't understand what they were saying or what they were doing. He must have told the others to pick up the Sheriff because that was what they did. I tried to stop them from touching him but one of them hit me in the side of the head with his gun butt end and I was out cold.

They put us on their horses and took us to their village. That's where I woke up at. It took some time for me to get my hearing back as I slowly come back to myself. When I got my eyes cleared up enough to where I could see straight. I was inside of a teepee and I was not there alone. There were some women that were tending to my head wounds. I knocked their hands away from my head and tried to see if the Sheriff was there with us. He was nowhere to be seen. That big tall Indian came through the flap door and into where we were at.

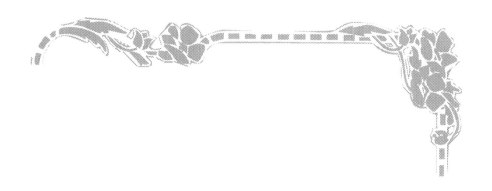

CHAPTER THREE

THE VILLAGE

He enter the teepee and walked over to where they had a bunch of skins in a pill and he sat down on top of them. He had to be somebody of great importance because those women stop tending to me and now they were tending to his every need. All that he had to do was just grunt and they jumped as if he had shot them.

I surely thought that my goose was cooked about right now. If they were planning on killing me, I sure wished they would go ahead and do it. The not knowing is about to kill me anyhow.

He sat there and just stared at me without saying a word. After staring at me for a while, he finally spoke to me and he asked if I had everything that I needed.

Something for my nerves wouldn't hurt about right now but instead of saying that to him I told him that I was fine. I just wanted to know about the Sheriff. I could understand him a little bit. He spoke English pretty good or, at least, well enough to where I could understand him.

He said that his name was "Silver Cloud." He was the "Chief of the Blackfoot tribe". "I asked him about the Sheriff?"

I told him that I wanted to see him if he was still alive. I told him that he was my best friend and I was really worried about him.

With one wave of his hand, he said no, not right now. He was with the "Shamans" and if the spirits wish for him to live he will.

I already knew what, the Shaman was. He is more or less a doctor. He had a great understanding of wild herbal roots, nuts and berries. He learned this from Shamans in the past. They always chose someone to take over for them when they got too old to do it themselves anymore. They would train them from a very young age. That way they would be ready when it came time for them to take over for the old Shaman. He used everything that he could to save your life.

The Indians was very religious. They believed that they came from Mother Earth. She was the most powerful Spirit that they had. The Shaman was invoking her Sprite to help heal the Sheriff.

This was the man that the Sheriff had come to find to start with, because he called him, just simply the Sheriff. He then told me this tell of when he first saw the Sheriff.

Silver Cloud said that he was out with a hunting party and he was thrown from his horse. The Sheriff had found me and keep me alive. It was in the winter when we first met. He feed me and took care of my broken leg. He taught me all about his world and I told him about ours. I told him how we lived and what we believed in. He had this shirt on that had a star on it with blue stripes running up and down the front of it.

It was a shirt that he would have been wearing if he was in the army. He must have been a deserter. There was so much about him that I didn't know and I didn't realize that until now. The Sheriff never talked about his past, not even with me. I do not even know the Sheriff's real name. I have been just like all the other people that knew him. We just knew him as the Sheriff.

When he had come to Maple Wood, he took the job of Sheriff and no one thought to ask him any questions about his past. That was the only thing that he asked of us and that was to never ask him nothing about where he had come from.

The Sheriff also said that you couldn't judge someone by where you have been but where they are going. That was all that really matter after all. He was the only one that wanted the job and that was good enough for us. We all thought that he would tell us after he had gotten to know us a little better.

The Sheriff taught me, how to speak like a White Man that winter and I taught him our language as well. He saved my life and now I shall have the Shaman to work the Sprites to return the favor of life, to him. I was the one that gave him the name Sheriff. I gave him that name when he was reborn. We spent the whole winter in his little cabin along for months. Then he brought me back to my tribe. I will always be in his debt. A life for a life. That is our way, the chief said. With him saying that he just stood up and went back outside of the teepee.

I wanted to leave with him but the other women wouldn't let me. They had been feeding me some kind of infusion of Pulverized leaves and some kind of Blossoms of Tansy, which help me with my dizziness and for me feeling so weak.

The women didn't talk near as good English as the Chief did but I could still make out most of what they were saying. Their job was to bear children and to gather wild roots, berries, and other useful plants for food and medical uses. They also were responsible for building Lodges, clothing and all the tools that they would need. Their lives were very active and physically demanding.

Women in this tribe had different ranks. Their higher status could be reached if they were part of an extended family with Distinguished Ancestors. It's about like politics in the White Man's world, it is not what you did but it is who you know that could get you out of the trouble that you had gotten yourself into.

The women here had to be hard working, chaste and modest. They also had to be skilled in the Tribe's Traditional Crafts. They also had to have great knowledgeable of their people and customs. If you were one of the lucky ones that asked for a Powwow for a Princesses and you was allowed to do so by the Chief. You were lucky because they were believed to be of higher power and standing in the tribe. The women had told me that the man that I called the Sheriff was in the Sweat Lodge. He would remain there for as long as the Spirits wanted him to be there.

They then told me, to not go near the Teepee that was smoking a lot, from the top. He was there with the Shamans and he was using Supernatural powers and with that and his curing powers and Techniques. He will do what he can for the Sheriff. He will be done with him when the smoke changes from black of the night to the red like a new sunrise of a new day.

Do not worry because in the Sweat Lodge where the Sheriff and the Shamans were at, is where he would use curing Techniques involving Herbal and Roots Remedies and Ritual Purification. They would burn wild roots and herbs and smoke as well as for prayer to invoke the Spirits. Death could be Natural or Spiritual. It was all up to him and the Spirit guides. "If they chose him to live he will but if the Death Spirit finds him he shall die."

It was as simple as that to them. That sounds cold but it was their way of coping with what life through at you.

"Tonight we shall dance the Dance of Life. That will help him keep the Spirit of Life. They said that they dance for a lot of reasons such as welcoming in the four seasons and for courting. There is also a dance for War Parties. They tanned their hides to make dresses and for clothing, shelters, and many other uses. They showed me some of their wedding clothing. They were died with wild berries and herbs. That made them breathtaking and they sewed in beads and colored stones. They were a site to behold."

If a warrior danced in one of the wedding clothes that they had made and the worrier danced over to you and if he put his arms around you and covered you with that gown. You were married for life. That's all it took. They did so much more like growing crops of corn and beans, squash, wild rice and tobacco. They were living a life that they could from nothing but what Mother Earth had given to them.

They also had ways of defending their self's, such as clubs, tomahawks, bows, and arrows. They even had lances and revolvers, rifles and shotguns. They had their own religion and culture as well as language. They had all that they needed to live the way they wanted to.

They were known to be great horse warriors because of their ability to ride their horses bareback. They were well known for their ability as protectors and providers as well for leaders. They could gain rank by doing various acts of bravery and performing various acts of great titles equal to what the Chief did, to get to where he was. I had to stay inside of that Teepee for two more days. Then I was allowed to go outside.

The women told me that I could walk around the tribe as long as I didn't bother anyone. They had work to do and I was there only as an honored guest. I was not to join in unless I was invited to do so.

I was for sure in a whole different world. They were running around just like they were lost but yet they knew exactly what they were doing. I walked around the tribe and I was blown away by the pure beauty of the tribe being a whole. They worked together as if they were a Well-Oiled Machine. What one had and the other one needed, they just took it without suffering any consequences.

"Why can't we do that," "I asked you?"

Sure they have their problems just like us but we take the some things too far. "The Bible says," "Eye for and Eye!"

We lock people up every day for crimes that they comment and then we fuss about the cost of locking them up. "Hell" some of them are locked up for life and we have to pay for it. I say that's not fair but there isn't anyone listening, to little old me.

"I was walking around and watching them when this woman came out of her Teepee and she had this big club in her hand. I was scared that she was coming for me but instead she turned and she stopped. She was watching some dogs that were running around her feet. Then she picked the fattest one out and with one mighty swing she killed it. The dog was jumping around on the ground while its nerves were dying. The other dogs ran for the hills."

"She reached down and picked that dog that she had killed up and she shook it at me and said something in her tongue. I didn't know what the words meant but I sure know what she was going to do with that dog. It was once running around and now it was what she was having for dinner."

"I hope that I wouldn't be expected to eat that dog. I don't care how she was planning on fixing it. It was still going to be a dog that she was eating. I think that I am going to be sick."

The Chief must have been watching me because he walked over to where I was standing there at just staring at what I had just seen.

"The Chief asked me" "if there was something wrong with what I had saw?"

I stood there in front of him and I couldn't say a word.

He said, don't judge before you know.

I just looked at him as he reached out and took me by the hand. He walked me over to one of the open fires that were burning. They had fires burning all the way around the tribe.

He sat down and reach out his hand and patted the ground beside him.

He wanted me to set down right beside of him on the ground. He had a story to tell me he said.

No sooner did we both set down. The women came out and draped us both with the softest deer skins that I had ever felt.

He said before the White Man come along. There was plenty of wildlife and fish as big as you or I, in the streams. The waters were as clean as the first-morning dew drops were. We all lived off the land and we were free, to be free. We were happy. Then White Man come and took from the land of plenty but didn't give back. They took too much. This made the Sprites angry. But the Sprites did nothing. They watched and they learned.

We take from the land only what we need and nothing more. We give thanks for the bloodshed so we can survive. The White Man does not. They only know how to take and they keep on taking. If we done as the White Man does, we would not know the cry of the great Eagle or the sight of a newborn Elk. The white man shoots first then he looks to see what he has killed. This is not the way of the Blackfoot Indians. We always use what we kill or we do not touch it. That is the way of the Spirits.

The man that you were found with was once a White Man that was taught that way before the Spirits touched his heart. The day that he found me was the first day of his new life, even if he didn't know that yet.

It was the day that I found my new brother. He could have killed me while I was laying there on the ground. I know that was what he had planned on doing but the Great Spirits touched his heart and he did not. Instead, he lost his hatred for the Indian and he saw me as an equal. He took my broken and half frozen body, back to that cabin in the woods.

He dressed my wounds just as you dressed his. He fed me just like you fed him. He washed me just like you washed him. He protected me just like you did him. I asked you one question know. "What is the difference between you and me?"

I didn't say a word I didn't know how. He was right. There were no differences between us. They were free and I was not. That was what he was trying to tell me. I had to pay for my supper and they didn't.

"The dogs would go hunger in the winter and starved to death, sooner or later. That women didn't do nothing wrong by killing that dog to eat. She was taking from the land to feed her family. For if she hadn't done that, the dog and her family would both go hunger tonight."

The wise Chief told me that when the Sheriff comes out of the sweat Teepee with the Shaman just like before, he will be a new man. "That's how he was born right the first time. That was the day that he become known as the Sheriff." "He was called that by our Shaman because of the star that he wore on his shirt." The chief had told me more about the man that both of us knew as just plainly, "the Sheriff," than what I had learned from him by myself, over the years that I knew him.

"I couldn't help but to ask myself," "who was really the man that we all knew as the Sheriff?"

"Where did he actually come from?"

"Should I ever ask him?"

I had so many questions to ask but you know, I don't really want to know any of the answers anymore. It's just not that important somehow. I knew him as the Sheriff and he had not changed, but I have. I have learned so much by this time of my life. I seemed to have a greater understanding of life and what is happening right under my nose.

"What can I say, I guess I'm a real slow learner?"

After we were done with our talk. I walked back around the tribe and this time, I had taken off my blinders. I could see so much better without them. I was now able to see the little things that I had been missing, for all of my life. I was reborn there by that fire with the Chief.

He had lifted the veil from my eyes. I could now hear the Squirrels running up and down the trees and the water hitting the big Boulders in the river. There was a Deer in the high grass, down by the river's edge and the wind blowing past me. I could stand still and watch the world keep on moving.

There was a belief that the Indians had, that when a child was born, Mother Earth gave it part of herself to use and when that baby grew old and the Death Spirit would take it back to her. What they meant was, that we was just here for a short time and we needed to slow down and enjoy the time that she had given to us. For when she decided to take it back, she would. How long that she let you keep it was not up to us but it has always been up to her and her alone.

I walked around the tribe and I saw the girls had braids in their hair. They had taken so much time with it that it was perfect. They had beads and colored grasses woven into their braids. They walk up so straight and with such pride in their selves.

I know had so much respect for them for what they had done for the Sheriff and myself.

I had figured out that, I was in love with that man and I found my heart, longing for him. I knew that they had told me not to go near the Teepee where he was but I couldn't help myself. I walked as close to the Teepee, as I dared. I was trying to see if there was some sign of life there. The smoke that was coming out of the top of the Teepee had somehow changed color. It was black and now it was red, almost like blood. The women were running around it as if it was on fire.

I took off towards the Teepee and the other women stopped me before I could enter it. The Chief told me that if I had entered the Teepee, the women would have killed me, right then and there. For their belief was that if a woman, were to enter the Shamans Teepee, without his permission, it would let the Evil Spirits out into the world.

The Teepee flap door opened and the Shamans came out of it and he said something to the Braves that was standing there.

I don't know what his words was but they went inside and brought the Sheriff outside back into the world once more. There he was, as each brave was holding him up by standing on both sides of him. Each one was holding one of his arms while given him their support. They let go of him and he was standing there on his own two feet. The only clothes that he had on was this little piece of hide that was covering his groin. He was colored up from head to toe with colored dye. He had every color that was in the rainbow all over his body. He was a site to behold.

I knew that he was the man for me. He looked as if he wasn't even from this world. There was nothing from this world that could do, any harm to him. He was untouchable. They walked him over to the Chief's Teepee. He stood there and all the young Braves ran up to him and they hit him with corn shucks. They were giving him their blessing. He was now reborn. He was truly a different man in my eyes, as well as for in their eyes also.

Some of the young braves started yelling and screaming, as well as dance around him as they moved him closer to the fire that they had built up to where it was going so high, that it looked as if it was flaming all the way up into the Heavens. They were dancing and hitting drums and chanting some sort of Spiral Racial while they were doing it. This went on all night long.

I still was not allowed to touch him and I really did want to fly into his arms. They were some women that came out of their Teepee just as the first morning razes, was just starting to come over the mountains tops and they draped some fancy painted skins that they had made onto his shoulders. It draped down and covered his entire body and drug the ground behind him as he was dancing around, while singing their songs, in their native tongue. He did this for a spell and then he danced around the fire and he came to a stop, right in front of me.

"We were now looking straight into each other's eyes. The song and the drums stopped when he did. He open his arm up as far and as wide as he could while standing in front of me. I jumped into his open arms in tears and he slowly closed the skins, slowly wrapping his arms around me. Then he kissed me and turned his head from me and he was now looking at the Chief."

"The Chief just nodded his head at him and he had this tall pole in his hand. The pole was painted up with bright colors and the spear at the top of it was draped with eagle feathers. He raised it up to the Heavens and then he hit the bottom of it, on the ground three times. Everyone in the tribe started to scream and shout, really loud. The Sheriff looked back at me and he gave me one more kiss."

"He asks me" "if I knew what had just happened?"

I told him that I didn't have a clue to what was actually happening.

"He said woman you are not alone no more, you are now my wife."

I didn't know what to say. The only thing that I wanted to say was what took you so long but nothing came out of my open mouth.

"He said that," "as long as he has known me," "I finally see that," "I have made you speechless." "Well," "miracles never seize" "the Sheriff said."

Before I could speak, the women in the tribe rushed us both into this Teepee that was colored up and decorated so beautifully and they closed the flap door behind us.

I was now a married woman and you know I could not have been able to plan a better wedding, even if I tried.

"I was happy and so was the Sheriff!"

CHAPTER FOUR

THE HONEYMOON IS OVER

We had been inside our honeymoon Teepee for five whole days and five nights. We had not left the Teepee the whole time. The Sheriff and I have not laid eyes on the outside world every sense we interred the Teepee. The women in the tribe had saw to our every need. That was their way of showing their respect to us now that we were married. We sure did enjoy our honeymoon and learning more about each other. That's why we were left inside the Teepee for five days and for five nights all alone.

We were to be separated from the outside world. No work nor could violence be allowed to enter that Teepee with us. We were not to lay our eyes on nothing but each other. I could have stayed there with the man that I loved forever but it was now time for us to join the outside world once more.

They had open the Teepee on the sixth morning and left it open. They just walked off after they open it and left us alone in the Teepee. They had invited us to reenter the outside world but they also left it up to us whenever we decided to do so.

The honeymoon was now over with. I was expecting them to be on the outside waiting for us to exit the Teepee, but they were nobody there to greet us. It was if we didn't matter to them anymore. "I asked" "the Sheriff," what was going on?"

He said that they only gave us five days and five nights to get to know each other and as far as they were concerned that was enough time for that. By the sixth morning, we should have learned everything about each other that we really needed to know. We had the rest of our lives to learn anything else that we needed to know about each other, which we didn't find out in our honeymoon Teepee. It was now time for us to join back with the outside world of the living. We had to live out here in the real world and what we did with our lives, from this time on, was up to us, not them. It was now up to us to find a way to live together. They don't believe in "divorce," so we are stuck to gather for all times.

They believe that even after death our Sprits will somehow find each other and join us back to gather, on the Milky Way. The stars that guided them throughout their lives, while they are alive will also reunite our soles together in the afterlife.

That's what they mean when they say that we have to give back what we had taken. They mean our bodies. It will rot and then return back to Mother Earth but our Sprits will rise up, into the Heavens. Our life was ours and their life was theirs. That was their way. We stayed there in the tribe with our new family, for two more days.

The Sheriff and I knew that it was time that we got on with our business. We sat down with the Chief and talked with him for a spell.

"The Sheriff and I ask him" "if he had seen anyone that had look to be, an outsider around these parts?

The Chief told us that he had heard for some of his hunting parties that someone had been staying up the river, in the next valley. They were staying in an old abandon hunting cabin that was up there high on a ridge.

The Chief told us that three White Men was staying there. They had been there for a little bit longer than when we had arrived in his valley. They are still there.

The Sheriff had told him that one of them was wanted for murder back in Maple Wood, where we had come from. We have been on their trail for some time now. That's what we were doing when that Mountain Lion attacked us.

The Chief said that's how we found you. When Hazel burned the infection out of your leg, you let out this loud cry of pain, which we heard from our tribe. That was why we tracked you down. I was pleased to find that it was you my brother and not some other White Man. Hazel, you done the right thing for my brother by burning out the evil Spirits. If you had not done that he would have surely died. That is why the Spirits of Mother Earth had brought you to us. You see there is nothing that happens without Mother Earth knowing about it first. We are all of one people.

"I would like to ask you for something my brother," the Sheriff" "asked the Chief?"

I would like for you to help us track down these bad White Men down and we shall see that the White Man's justice is done. The man that killed the other man back in Maple Town shall pay for what he had done, with your help.

The Chief said brother, we shall help each other. They are taking from Mother Earth and they are not giving back. We shall track him down for you and then we shall give him to you, for the crimes that he has done against your kind and Mother Earth. Rest for one more night and by morning, we shall have the men in our site the Chief told us.

We stayed there in the tribe for that night but we were on the rise before the sunlight came over the high Mountain top. We were on our horses and on the trail of the bad men, very early the next morning. We had found the valley that the cabin was in.

The Chief had told us to stay back and to let his best Trackers go in front of us. They were going to see, what they could and only they know how to see without being seen. "They had gotten into position when they called out like a bird, would have." "Their way of talking to each other was by sounding like the wildlife that was all around us, all the time. You wouldn't think twice about hearing a crow hollowing or an owl." I watch and I learned so much from them.

They had sent for us to come closer to the hunting cabin where the bad guys were staying at. The Trackers that the Chief had sent out first were hidden on all four sides of the cabin by the time that we had gotten there but I still couldn't see the first one of them. They are sure knew what they were doing. "Those men didn't even know what was about to come down upon their heads."

One of the Braves snuck up to the cabin close enough to where he could throw little pebbles and hit the door with them. He did this twice before someone came outside. They waited until they had stepped away from the front door, far enough so they could take him out without alarming the others.

They jumped him as soon as he round the corner of the cabin. I was right there and I saw everything but yet I heard nothing. They had him down and he was out. "Well, one down and two to go."

This time, they did something entirely different. This time, they let one of their horses lose and they made sure that it ran right passed the front of their door. It worked like a charm. Sure enough one of them took off after that horse, just as soon as they saw it. They were waiting for him and they jumped him to, without making a sound. "Two down and one to go."

The last man was still asleep in his bed. He had no idea, what was about to happen to him. He sure didn't hear them coming. He was asleep when they jumped him and they gave him a rude awakening. "Before he could even react," "he was theirs."

They had caught all three of them and not the first sound nor a shot was even fired. They had all three of them and they looked so confused. They saw all those Indians all around them and I knew, that they wouldn't hurt them but you couldn't convince them of that, with the looks that the Indians were giving them. They were just waiting to be scalped, about any moment now. The Sheriff and I walk up to them and they were sure at a loss for words by now. They didn't expect to see the likes of us, way out here, not to say anything about the Indians.

The Sheriff walked up to them and introduced himself and he told them why we were out there looking for them. They, of course, denied even being in Maple wood. They said that we were just wasting our time by being there.

The Sheriff told them that he was not going to agree with them. He would let the evidence speak for them. I just see what I can find and he walked right by them into the cabin.

He was in there for just a short time, when he come out with some money and some dope. The money was in a money bag still and it had the town banks name on it.

"He walked up to them and he ask them," "how are you three going to explain this to me?"

They looked at each other and starting to deny the whole thing. The Sheriff said that he was looking for just one man. Not three men.

Two of them looked at each other and then those two turned their heads and looked straight at the last man.

The Sheriff knew then who he had to talk to. The other two let the cat out of the bag.

The Sheriff walked over and stood right in front of that young man.

The Sheriff must have looked ten feet tall to him, I say.

The man still didn't own up to the murder or to why he had so much money with them. He could not explain why the money was in one of our town's bank bags either.

The Sheriff asked, him about the dope and he denied that as well.

The Sheriff just looked at the Chief and he said, that he had found, what he come for, so they could have them to do with as they wanted to.

The Chief said that he would take care of them for us.

"The Sheriff just walk over to where I was standing and he asked me" "if I was ready to leave?"

He said that he had what he come for. Since they were not willing to tell him about the murder that happen in town, then he had no use for them. No sooner did the Sheriff say that.

The young Braves jumped on top of those three men and they drew their knives out and acted as if they were going to skin them alive. The young Braves was yelling and screaming as they were doing it. They acted as if they were out of their minds.

I felt sorry for those three men as the Sheriff took me by the arm and we started to walk off. Now it didn't take them but a few seconds for them to begin to talk. "Heck, they were petrified of those Indians." They just didn't know which one was going to speak the loudest when those Indians had gotten done with them.

They told the Sheriff to stop them from killing them and they would tell him anything that he wanted to know. The Sheriff looked sideways at me and he wink his right eye just so I could see him doing it, then he turned around and said, that they better not leave out nothing. He said that he wanted to hear the truth and nothing but the truth from them. I won't asked you for no details, so don't leave anything out.

They started to spill their guts as fast as they could.

They told us that the man that was killed in the camp grounds name was Mike Jones and worked at the bank. He had robbed the bank and he was dropping off the money to Jed.

His name is really Jed Hall. Jed is our younger brother.

Jed was there at the campground and he killed Mike so we didn't have to cut him in on the money and split the money four ways. Jed did it and he stole a horse and he was supposed to meet us, here at the cabin. We were going too waited here for things to die down for a while. Then we were going to cross over the Mountain top and go north into Canada. There we would be home free.

"The Sheriff asked them," "how did they get the man that they killed to go along with their plan?"

They were going to pay him his part of the money and give the drugs to him to sell as well. Jed had a change of heart and Jed decided to cut our losses and keep all the profit for ourselves. We were afraid that Mike Jones would get caught while trying to sell that Marijuana and tell on us. That was another reason why he had to go.

That's good enough for me the Sheriff said.

"What about you Hazel," "the Sheriff ask her?"

Yes, my dear, I said, that's good enough for me too. The Sheriff and I thanked the Chief and all the young Braves that had caught them all for us and they help us get the pensioners ready for the long ride back to town and we left that same day.

CHAPTER FIVE

THE LONG RIDE BACK

We had a long way to go before we were going before we would be home. All five of us were dreading the trip back home but what could I say, we still had to go. You have to start somewhere and for the five of us it starts right here.

I was more than willing to stay there with my new family. I knew that was not their way and they welcome us but they would not let us stay there forever in peace with them. That was their home, not ours. It was their ways and not the White Man's way. They did all that they were supposed to do for us, now the rest was up to the Sheriff and myself and nobody else.

We were now on our on and we were so happy. I was now a wife and my eyes were finally open. I know that the Sheriff was happy because, he couldn't smile no bigger, even if he tried.

The Sheriff had all of us riding in single file so that he could keep his eyes on all of us, myself included. We were going through the narrow pass, where we had that encounter with that Mountain Lion.

When we rode up to that spot, where the Lion had attacked us, I couldn't help but to stare at it. The little shelter that I had made was still there. It had been torn down by our Indian friends when they first found us, but in my eyes, it look the same way as when I first built it. That was the place that I had to keep my best friend alive. That place was now burned into my memory forever.

You could see that Mountain Lions corpse still lying off to the side of where we was and all the blood stained ground had now turned black. The Indians had taken its hide off of its body for their own personal use. They didn't like to waste nothing especially if they could find a use for it. Otherwise, it would have gone to waste.

I could still see it as a plan in my mind as if it had just happened. It was as fresh in my memory as if I was still there and it had just happened. I could still smell the burning of the Sheriff's flesh as I put that red hot spoon into his cut, on his leg. I guess somethings you are not supposed to forget and that places and what had happened there, was one for me.

The horse's ears were moving from side to side, so that meant that they didn't séance any danger and we made it through the pass without any trouble at all. I could now breathe, a little bit easier.

The Sheriff told us that we would keep on driving the horses as far and as fast as we could. He was aiming at getting home as quick as possible. We rode hard for the next few days and we were now almost ready for us to reenter the big open meadow of never ending high grass.

We made camp just at the edge of the open meadow. There was water and the horse could pick the grass that was growing there. That way they could keep up their strength for the rest of the trip home.

We had the horses feet hobbled and the three men's hands were tied up. The Sheriff had tied their legs to each other's so they couldn't try and run away from us. We made camp there and the Sheriff and I took turns keeping watch, throughout the night.

The daylight was starting to cut its way across the open sky when we broke camp the next morning. The Sheriff told everyone that we was going to enter the high grassy meadow and we was to just walk the horses slowly through the grass. Listen to what I am saying to you and don't try to run your horses for no reason so whatever. There could be anything out there hiding in that tall grass, so keep your wits about you. We should get to the other side without any trouble. He wanted to go first and then we all would follow behind him in single file. Keep a close eye on the ground in front of you and watch your horse's ears as well. They will smell the danger before you can see it coming.

There he goes again putting himself back in harm's way this time for all of us as he took the lead.

The horses started to go through the giant sea, of nothing but endless high grass. That seemed to never stand still, as the wind tossed it from side to side. Then the horses started to act up a little at first but then they acted up a bit more, as we got further and further into the tall grass. "They were scenting some kind of danger was out there waiting for us." We couldn't see anything but there was something out there in the grass.

We had no way of knowing what, so we just pressed on towards home. We walked our horses very slowly and we were all watching the ground for whatever we could see. There was something out there, that's for sure. Because the horses and all of us could feel the danger, that we were all in. You could look just up ahead and see that the tall grass was coming to an end. We were just about through the grass when, out of nowhere, you could hear a scary sound, that none of us wanted to hear, especially when you couldn't see it.

It was a rattle sound that came from but one place. The tail of a big "Rattle Snake".

From the sound of it. It must have been a big one because the horses were in a pure panic because of the sound that it was making. The horses had the sound of that Rattle Snake in their ears. They couldn't see the ground clearly either and that made them very uneasy. They were out of control and their first instinct was to run.

The Sheriff was in front and he yelled back to me, in the back of the line. "That he could hear the snake but he couldn't find it." It is close he said, so everybody be careful and try to control your horses, the best way that you can. He said, that and he went on ahead and then the next two made it through without too much trouble.

Jed was in front of me and he was young and stupid, because he would not listen to me or what the Sheriff had told him. I had told him to just follow the same path that the others had already made but he didn't listen to me. He did the one thing that you should never do. "He let his fear get the best of him."

He kicked his horse and he let that snake get the best of him and he went to fast through the tall grass. He didn't follow the same trail that the other horses had already made through the grass. He was going too fast to watch the ground in front of himself.

Sure enough, he ran right up on top of that snake and it struck out at his horses legs. The horse reared straight up with him on its back and threw him off and he hit the ground hard. He had landed right beside that snake and it done just as nature had designed it to do.

"It struck out at him as his horse ran off in the other direction. It bit him right in the face. It hit him in his left eyeball while sinking its fangs deep down into his eye. With that one strike, it had busted his left eyeball and then it quilted back up like a spring and struck him again. This time, it hit him in the side of his check. Just about besides his left ear. It was bad and we all knew it and so did Jed."

I rode my horse over to where he was and before the snake could strike him for the third time, I shot it, killing the snake. "The damage was already done." He was in a great deal of pain due to the amount of venom that the snake had pump into his face. Jed was now dying and there was nothing that we could do to stop that from happening. There was nothing that none of us could do but watch helplessly as he took his last breath.

The snake was a big one and it sunk all of its venom into Jed's face. He had paid a high price for doing wrong. If he had not chosen a life of crime, he would not be out here, with that snake, to start with. He was now giving back, what Mother Earth had given to him, his life force.

"There was nothing for us to do but to catch his horse and tie his lifeless body on the back of it and continue on our way. We were all sorry but what else could we do. Jed had done all this to himself and he did pay the price."

The Sheriff was trying to do the right thing by taking his body back to town so his family could have so peace of mind and bury him. This way they would have some sort of closure. We still had about four more days' worth of hard riding yet to do before we were going to be home. We all just hoped that nothing else would go wrong before we got there.

We have been back on the trail for two days now and all is well, I am pleased to say. That day we rode the horses harder than all the other days put to gather. We all wanted to sleep in our own beds instead of that hard ground. I was still glad when the Sheriff had said, that it was time for us to make camp where we were at, for the night.

He always tried to stop close to where we would have water and the horse would be able to feed as well. We had built up another camp fire and the Sheriff had shot us some Squirrels for supper. I was not alone, when I tell you, that we were all tired of Beef Jerky by this time. I put the Squirrels on long sticks and laid them on the fire so they would cook.

We were just sitting there making small talk when the horses started to act up once more. This time, they were trying to run off.

"The Sheriff said that something was trying to spook them. He said, this time, he knew what that was, it's Wolves."

They wanted the horses to run wild so that they could separate them from each other. Then they would surround one of them and take it down.

The Sheriff told us that we must do as he asked and for us not to question him when he told us to do something. Then he walked over to the two boys and he cut them lose.

"I jumped up to my feet and ask him," "what in the world are you doing Sheriff?"

He said, for me to hush. If we are going to make it through this night, we all have to work together. He turned and look at the two that he had just set free and he said to them. If you want to run then run, but I won't be stopping you but that Wolfpack that is surrounding us right now will stop you thought. So go ahead and run if you dare.

They knew that the Sheriff would not lie and they were not going anywhere. I am not going to give you your guns back because I done gave them to the Indians that help catch you before we left their tribe. I have a Riffle and so does Hazel. Stay close to us and do everything that I tell you and just maybe we will all make it through the night together. They told him that they would not try to escape and they would listen to every word that he said.

The horses, go and get them, Hazel. Get them as close to the fire as they will let you put them. I want you two boys to look for as much firewood as you can possibly find before it gets too dark. The night is when they will do us in if they can. As long as we all stick together, we all should be just fine.

So we all did, just as the Sheriff had said. We worked together and got everything done just as the Sheriff had instructed us to do so. We put the horses close to the fire and we built the fire up really high.

The Sheriff told us that they won't to attack us as long as the fire stays high. Regardless of what happens, don't let the flames die down. They will wait until the fire dies down, in the middle of the night and that's when they will come for us. That's when they will strike. Regardless of what happens, don't go out into the dark of the night. Keep our backs towards each other's, at all times.

The Sheriff did something next that I know he really didn't want to have to do. He walked over to the horse that still had Jed's body tied on him and he cut the rope that was holding him up on the saddle. His dead body flopped to the ground as if it was no more than a sack of feed.

"The Sheriff told the other two boys, to help him and they carried Jed's body out into the dark of the night. He took it about as far as he dared to go and he threw it down on the ground. They walked backward, back to the safety of the fire. He had feed Jed's dead body to the Wolves. He told us that might keep them from attacking us in the middle of the night. Then he looked at me and I could tell by the look that he had in his eyes that it wouldn't."

The Sheriff and I were the only ones that had guns and he told me not to waste the shells if I didn't have too.

He knew that my aim was true but the other two didn't really know me at all. They were scared for their lives and so was the Sheriff and I. Sam and Will Hall was the other to boy's names. We had always been able to make small talk ever time that we stopped for the night but this time, nobody was saying a word. We just sat there by the fire and keep on listing to the sounds of the wolves tearing into Jed's body. They were fighting and making all kinds of noises as they feed on his body.

There was no way of knowing how many of them that were really out there in the night. It sounded as if there was an army of Wolves was just waiting for us to let our guard down.

The night creep by slower and slower. Morning just couldn't get here fast enough for us. It had been about two hours since the boys and the Sheriff had taken Jed's body and feed it to the Wolves and they were calming down somewhat. They were not making near as much noise as they had at first.

Sam said that they were getting quite so that must mean that they are going to leave us alone.

The Sheriff said that's not the way they hunt. They are sizing us up as we speak. They already know who they are going to take out first. They are a pack animals. That means that they will hunt only as a pack. They take their prey out by working together.

"The Wolves were getting braver, as the night wore on. They were trying to get the horses to break free and run out into the night, to where only death awaits them. We were running low on wood and the fire was starting to burn lower. The flames were all that was keeping them at bay for now."

The Wolves found out that the horses were not going to break free and run off, so they must have come up with another plan of attack. The wolves were running right up to the edge of where we were. They had an easy meal just on the other side of the darkness, towards the light of the campfire. They had every intention of getting it.

We were using big sticks and we were also throwing rocks and screaming as loud as we possibly could.

The more noise, the better the Sheriff yelled out.

We were trying to stay alive and they were attempting to end our lives. We were going to have to battle for our lives for the rest of the night. That was where we stood at this time.

Will and Sam's nerves were on edge as well as the Sheriffs and for me. We were exhausted and we wanted this nightmare to stop.

The Wolves had now started to come out of the night and now they were coming right into our camp.

"The Sheriff said that for me to open fire on them. Make them Riffle shells count for something Hazel the Sheriff yelled out to me. Hazel, my love, make them little Devil dogs, earn their supper."

So I open fire and the wolves, never even slowed down.

They had picked out their victim and they were going to get it regardless of the cost.

"Before we knew it, they had Will by his legs and they jerked his feet out from underneath of him. They were about four of them that had hold of him and they were dragging him out into the night."

"Will was yelling for us to help him but we already had our hands full and there was nothing that we could do for him. The Sheriff and I couldn't stop them. We were firing our guns as fast as we could but that wasn't even slowing them down one bit."

"The Sheriff did the only thing that he could to help Will out. The only thing that the Sheriff was able to do was to shoot him in the head. The Sheriff killed Will to save him from his fate."

It might have sounded like he had done a bad thing but he kept him from feeling the pain of the Wolves tearing his body apart. He had ended his life before the Wolves could. Will was their target and they was not going to stop until they had him and they didn't.

The morning light was now starting to brighten things up. That stopped the Wolves for now. After that night had ended, we all said, that we would ride the horses as hard as we could towards home.

The Sheriff told us that the Wolves would follow us all the way home, just waiting for that next meal so he was not planning on stopping for nothing. He didn't have to tell us that but once, for us to agree with his way of thinking.

We threw everything that we didn't need away so the horses could run as fast as they could. There was no way that we were going to slow down at night again. We rode the horses all night and rested a little while through the day and then we were right back into the saddle again heading for home. We made it home in record time.

I think that Sam was even glad to be locked up behind the cell bars of his jail cell. No Wolfs or Snakes or even Indians could get him now. He was finally feeling safe from all the wild thing that go bump in the wild.

The Sheriff and I walked over to the Diner and we eat our dinner like we had not eaten a meal for weeks. It was so good to feel like a stuffed turkey for Thanks-giving.

"We'll let us see the Sheriff told the Mayor James as he asked the Sheriff" "what had happened to us on this trip?"

He told them all about it and he left one part out as he stood up from his favorite table and he walk over to where I was sitting and held his hand out for mine to help me to my feet. When I had done that he finally told them that we were now married and as far as he was concerned he was still on his honeymoon and he didn't want to be disturbed as he walked himself and me up the stairs on the way to our bedroom. He looked back at me and he said, that's how you are supposed to leave them, Hazel. Speechless until next time.

"I'll have to let you know what he meant by that the next time that we go on a case, but for now, we have some homework to get to!"

"Don't worry too much about it, I get back to you really soon because crime doesn't ever stop, not even for me!"

"See you soon, love Hazel and the Sheriff!"

BOOK NUMBER THREE

HAZEL AND THE SHERIFF NEW LIFE TOGETHER

Hazel and the Sheriff new life together. That's the name of this third book in a series of tells that Hazel had me write. This wild tell that Hazel is going to tell you is back in the mid forty's and fifty's. People still used horses more than cars. They all live in a small outpost town called Maple Wood. It sets just on the outer skirts of Yellow Stone Nation Park. Hazel is the one that is telling this and other tells to you.

You just wait and you'll see that you really will like her. Hazel is a lady in her mid to early forty's. She is a real pistol. She doesn't care what she says or who she says it to. Hazel doesn't give a rat rump whether they like what she has to say or not because she is going to still say it. She is not afraid of nothing. "Man nor beast." The best shooter for miles around. She is the boss and she likes it that way. You will like all of her wit and her sharp personality. She is the one that is telling this story to you. I am just the writer.

You will love her fancy sayings and her wild side. Hazel is married to the Sheriff and although he might be the sheriff and have his own way of solving crime in our part of the world. They work well together but they sure don't see "eye to eye" all the time. Listen to the story that Hazel is telling you this time. See for yourself if she doesn't draw you into the day that her town got its black eye. The way that the Sheriff and Hazel tell this tale of horror will leave you asking how one man can kill hundreds of families and use his own child to help do it.

The main charter in this story is for sure a whole different kind of evil. Listen to the story as only the Sheriff and Hazel can only tell it to you. See if you agree to how the whole town got their revenge. You will love this story of shame and mistrust. How they all work together to bring their men to justice and what kind of justice that they take out on the evil parties in this tale that Hazel is telling to you. So I am telling you to hang on to your seat and let her tell you all about this story. See if you don't agree to what they were left no other choice but to do. That is the hardest part about having a choice to make, sometimes you just don't have that choice and you just have to do the right thing, whether you want to or not. You can only hope that you have made the right choice.

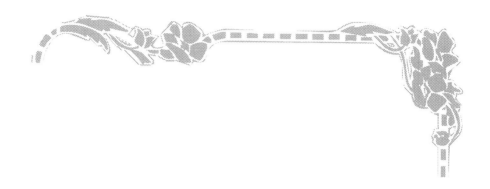

CHAPTER ONE

HAZEL AND THE SHERIFF'S NEW LIFE TOGETHER

The Sheriff and I were enjoying the day together so far and it had been almost two week's sense we had returned from Silver Clouds tribe. He was the blood brother of my husband the Sheriff. We had been just enjoying each other's company, ever since we had made it back to town, from where we had solved our last case. Even Sam Hall was just fine sitting over there in his Jail Cell at the Jailhouse.

We set off looking just for one man on that trip and we found three men. All of us didn't make the journey back home alive, though. We lost two of Sam's brother on the way back home. One from a big Rattle

Snake bite and the other one, the Sheriff had to shoot him in the head before the Wolves took his life from us.

Just think that we went through "Hell" for weeks just because of one man's need for murder. If Jed had not killed Mike Jones down at the Camp Grounds and took all the money and drugs for himself, we would have never had that murder to solve and Sam Hall would still have both of his brothers.

That just goes to show you that the Indians was right when they told me to learn how to respect time. They said that we need to slow down and enjoy what time that Mother Earth had given to us, for when she called your life force back to her, it shall go and there isn't nothing that you can do to stop that from happening. They had told me that it was up to her and nobody but her. What we did with the time that she had given to us, was up to us, though. If we wasted the time allotted to us by her then, "O well."

We were just sitting there enjoying the day, just as I had told you when bullets starting fly through the air. Someone was robbing the bank just down the street from my Diner. The bullets were cutting a path through the Diner's windows.

Everyone had hit the floor and dunk for cover. Everyone but me that is.

Hazel the Sheriff said, get down on the floor before someone shoots you.

I was on the other hand, "extremely pissed off."

"I said, "O' no they didn't."

That was just "enough to make me mad as hell," when they shoot out my big front picture windows. "How dare they I said."

I was outside on the front porch in a matter of seconds.

Hazel you stupid old woman the Sheriff yelled at me.

"What do you think that you're doing talking to me like that," "I yelled back inside to the Sheriff?"

"I turned and I fired a warning shot at my husband."

There was a bottle of whiskey sitting on the bar so I hit it and it shattered all over the Sheriff. Drowning his head in spilled whiskey.

"He asks," "what was that for?"

That's because your trousers are too tight or something is cutting your blood flow off to your brain if you think that you will ever get by with talking to me like that.

The Sheriff said that he was sorry for what he had said to me.

I just let him know to never let that kind of talk come out of his mouth again or next time it won't be a warning shot. Some people like to beat around the bush but I am a little more direct than that. I believe in getting my point across the first time and he knew that about me. It's not my fault that he forgot that.

The Sheriff was waiting around for me to say that I was sorry.

I told him that "people in Hell wants ice water too" but that wasn't going to happen either.

I turned my attention back to the bank robbers and there was about four of them on horseback fleeing from the bank.

The streets were like we were living in some sort of ghost town because everyone had run for cover, but I was not afraid of them. The men folk was all hidden and I was the only one that didn't hide from all the gun fire. "I was too pissed off" that they had shot my windows out to hide from them now. I was going to make them pay for it. I reached down and grabbed both of my guns. "I was planning on sending them to their maker by express mail, but I didn't have any more shells left in my guns."

I had just one shell left, that was in my guns and I had wasted it on that man that I married. I had been cleaning them when the gunfire started. I had taken the shells out of my guns and laid them on the table top that we were sitting at. When the men ran under them like mice, they must have knocked them off the top of the table and onto the floor. I couldn't do nothing as they just road right down the street right by me standing on my front porch as if I wasn't even standing there to start with. What they don't know is that I got a close look at every one of them.

One of them was riding a painted horse that was marked up with red and white body colors. There was one that was riding a horse that had a saddle that had a silver saddle horn on it.

I was so mad when they had done that, all I wanted to do was take it out on someone. "Hell anyone will do, so no one better not get in my way."

I walked back inside of the Dinner and I told the men that they were safe now and they could come out from under the table tops.

I looked at the Sheriff and he tried to make me feel sorry, about taking that pot shot at him but with one look at me, he knew that he was wasting his time. I was the best shot in these parts and my aim was true and he knew that if I wanted him dead, he would be!

"I could put up with a whole lot but don't ever try and disrespect me. That kind of action may cut your lifespan very short."

"The Mayor James" "asked the Sheriff and myself," "was we going to be able to get them all because they were four of them?"

I walked over to the Mayor and I told him, "I know that it doesn't sound fair to them, but that he could count on it." When we do get them, James, I told him, they will pay dearly for shooting out my picture windows.

I told the Sheriff to get ready and we will go to the bank and find out what we can there and then we will go and get them all. I walked over to where my bullets were laying on the floor and the Sheriff and the Mayor picked them all up and gave them back to me. I reloaded my guns and we were out the door heading towards the bank.

"I tell you more about all of us but I am still pissed off because of what those four dumb, want to be gunfighters, had done to my Diner." They will pay for that, so you will just have to follow along and find out how they do that. The Sheriff and I solve all the crime that happens around here. We are the only law that our part of the world, has to offer. We always get our man or in this case men.

We made it to the bank and I was shocked to find out, that they were more than four of them. They were six in all. Two of which had been gunned down, there inside of the bank. They also had shot the bank teller but he would live through it. The two that was shot there inside of the bank was shot by their on men. It didn't make since to why they would kill their on men like that but they did. The two men were outsiders and no one knew anything about them. I couldn't help but to wonder why they would hit the bank in our town when we didn't keep a whole lot of money there at any time. That's something that everybody should know.

"I asked the bank teller," "why did they want to still the money that we had in the bank, in our little town?"

His name was Peyton Lynn and he told me, that there were just a few thousand dollars in the safe but that was not what they were really after. They wanted the land titles more than the money, which we were keeping in the bank vault with the money that we had. That was what they kelp asking me for Hazel, so I gave them all to them along with the money. They had what they had come for and they said, that they wouldn't shoot me but they lied.

They shot the other two men Peyton said, in the face before either one of them could even move. They didn't even see it coming. They just turned and shot them both, like it wasn't nothing to them. I knew that they must have been afraid that someone might be able to identify them and that's why they had shot them both, in the face. That's the only reason that I can come up with for them doing such a thing. It was to stop us from ever finding out anything about them. We can't check the Sheriff's wanted posters and look for their faces, because thanks to them, shooting them in the face, they are now unrecognizable.

"The Sheriff asked Peyton," "what was so important with those land deeds, that was worth taking a chance on dying for?"

Peyton told us that, if the Sheriff and I wanted to know the answer to that question, we would have to go asked Mr. Donald.

Mr. Donald Macqueen was the richest man in our parts. He was stuck up and he always thought that his crap didn't stank. "There is nothing wrong with being rich" "but when you act the way that he did on account of his money," "yes sir," "that's what makes it wrong!"

"I was about to let him know that his crap did stink and if he didn't believe me when I tell him that, I think that it does and if he wanted me to, I'd show him."

The talk in the town was that the Railroad was planning on making a stopover, just outside of our town. Whoever owned that land was about to become very wealthy, that is if the tales that were going around town, was to be proven correct. That would explain why someone would still the land deeds to start with. If they knew who owned the land to start with, they would be able to buy it and then resale it to the Railroad at a large profit.

We now knew why and we had someone to ask. This case was turning out to be like all the rest for the Sheriff and myself. Wild and full of mystery, just the way that we like them. We will get to the bottom of this case and we would find out, why land was worth killing those two for and leaving them dead in the bank for us to find.

I don't bother no one and no one is going to bother me, that's for sure. That just the way that I am. They had done went and pissed me off, so all that I have to say is, we are coming for them and I bet we get them.

The Sheriff and I saddled up our horses and we set off to see Mr. Donald Macqueen after talking to Peyton. He lived just a little ways outside of our town and we were riding the horses hard to get there. I was trying to calm down but it has never been easy for me to control my temper.

We made it to Donald's ranch and sure enough, there in the corral with the other horses, was that red and white painted horse that, I had seen earlier. I knew then that he had something to do with the bank heist. I just had to find out why someone like him with all of his money would hire someone to rob our bank.

Mr. Donald Macqueen was sitting on the front porch as if there was nothing wrong. He was not fooling me, though. I knew that he was behind this but without more evidence, other than that horse in the corral. I couldn't arrest him. We got off our horses and tied them up to his hitch post and walk over to where he was.

"Mr. Donald Macqueen ask" "us both," "to take a set?"

I walked over to where he was and I sat down along with the Sheriff. We just sat there and made small talk for a while. Then I couldn't take it no more.

"I asked him," "about the red and white horse that he had in the corral?"

He said that he just bought that horse off some good old boys, which were passing through. Mr. Donald Macqueen said that they were in need of the money and he like the looks of the horse and the saddle so he bought them both.

That is when I told him about, what had happened earlier in town.

Donald, of course, denied knowing anything about it. Donald had this sideways smirk on his face and all that I wanted to do was smack it off of his face. I told him sense, he didn't know nothing about what I had already said to him.

"Then" "I asked him" "if he minded if the Sheriff and I could have a tour of his place?"

Mr. Donald Macqueen said, yes mam, look all you want to. He said that he didn't have anything to hide and he would love to give us all, the tour around his ranch.

The first place that he took us was through the barn and sure enough, there was that saddle which had a silver saddle horn on it, just sitting there on the floor of the saddle house.

I was in the right place and there was now no doubt in my mind. I knew that he had something to do with this whole thing. I still couldn't arrest him and the bad thing about it was, that he knew it too. When I walked over to where the saddle was and I pointed out that silver saddle horn.

Donald just got so quiet and he grew red in the face. He knew then that I knew that, he had something to do with what had happened there at the bank, in town.

When I tried to ask him some more questions about the bank robbery, he stopped me and denied knowing anything about it, of course.

Donald said that he had bought the painted horse and the saddle with the silver saddle horn was on the horses back when he bought the horse. He had bought them both for one price.

He was a slick one but although we couldn't arrest him for being so slimy, he knew that we knew. The next move was now up to him.

There was nothing else that we could do at that time, so we left. On the way back to town, I told the Sheriff everything that I had saw, as he rode by me when I was standing there on my front porch. I saw that painted horse go by and that silver saddle horn that was on that saddle, which he had in the barn. The only differences were the saddle was not on the painted horse but it was on one of the other horses backs.

The Sheriff said that he had an answer for everything that you ask him, Hazel. He knew that he was lying but there was nothing they could do about it for now. We need to get more evidence and we would see where the evidence would take us when we get it. We will get them, Hazel, you just wait and see if, I am not telling you the truth.

I just smiled and then I tried to calm myself down some more. I needed to get my head wrapped around all of this. I had a lot of questions to ask and if I ask them I knew that, I would not stop until I got the right answers to those questions.

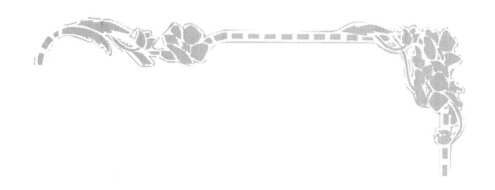

CHAPTER TWO

THE EVIDENCE

The Sheriff and I had made it back to the Diner and we started gathering all the evidence together. We know, the Sheriff said, that they were seven of them that robbed the bank in all. They robbed the bank but they were not after the money but the land deeds instead. Two of the men was killed there at the bank by their own men. They were shot in the face to hide their true identity from us. We know that the bank teller Peyton made sure to point out the fact that they were shot in the face so we would not be able to check my wanted poster to find out who they really were. They shot the bank teller but they could have killed him but they just wounded him instead. Mr. Donald Macqueen knows something but he is not saying. The painted horse and the saddle with the silver saddle horn were at the stables of Mr. Donald Macqueen. They made a big to-do about robbing our little bank, just to hide their real intent. I think that's all that we have for now to go on but we have some questions to ask and when we get the answers to those questions, we will have them all in jail with Sam. He has been there by himself for long enough, Hazel said.

"The questions that we have to answer now is" "who shot out my picture window's and who's going to pay me, for that?"

"Why did they pick our bank to rob" "and how did they know what day to rob the bank?"

"What does those land deeds have to do with anyone other than the rightful owners of the land?"

"Who are the real owners of the painted horse and that saddle with the silver saddle horn?"

"Why did they shot those two in our bank in the face to hide who they truly were from us?"

"Why did they shoot the teller" "but didn't kill him?"

"Why did the bank teller go to great links," "to point out why they shoot those two in the face?"

"Why did they use six men, just to knock off our little bank?"

"Who is really Mr. Donald Macqueen" "and what is he hiding?"

We had all the pieces to the puzzle now. All we had to do was link them together. The Sheriff and I were heading back over to the bank to see if there was anything that we might have overlooked. When we got there to the Bank, the Sheriff had already sent for the bank teller Peyton, to come back to the bank so he could help us reacted where everyone was standing at when the bank was robbed.

The young man's name was Payton Lynn. He was well known by all of us here in town. He has been working for the bank, for about two years now. He was married to Jamie. She was a sweet young lady and they had been married for about two years now.

We didn't know too much about her, though. He had gone on vacation two years ago and he came back as a married man. He had gone to New York and that was when he had met her, he told us. They fell hopelessly in love at first sight and was married right off, Peyton told us.

When the Sheriff asked him, about his world wind romance. He would answer the Sheriff but he keep his responses, short and to the point. He didn't describe nothing or go into any details of their relationship, as if he was holding back, for some reason or another. He should have been proud of the way that they met and ready to brag about their romance but instead, he keep quiet about it.

I didn't think too much about it at first but there was something wrong with the way that he was answering the Sheriff's questions, which bother me. He was hiding something and I knew it. You could tell because of his body language. He wouldn't look the Sheriff nor I, into our eyes. Yep, he was guilty of something, that's for sure.

The Sheriff had asked him, to tell us where he was standing when the bank was being robbed?

He said that he was behind the counter working as usually. That was his workstation. He waited on some customers and whenever they had left, that's when they came into the bank. He knew that they were strangers to our town because he had not seen them around our neck of the woods before.

"The Sheriff asked him," "who was the people that he had waited on before they had come into the bank?"

He said that he couldn't remember who they were.

"How many of them was there to start with," "the Sheriff ask him?"

He said that there was four of them that come inside of the bank and then two of them went back outside to stay with the horses.

Peyton had just told the first lie to the Sheriff. If you were working at a bank and someone robbed it, you sure would remember how many of them they were. That's one part that you wouldn't get wrong.

"The Sheriff," "ask Peyton," "why didn't their actions strike him as being odd?"

Penton answered the Sheriff and said, it just didn't occur to me as being odd. I was so busy at the time and I guess, I was not really thinking.

Penton was "sweating bullets" as the Sheriff keep walking around him and he keeps his eyes on Peyton the whole time. That was making Peyton "extremely nerves". He was rattled by what the Sheriff was doing and you sure could tell that he had a secret that was tearing him up inside.

I walked over to him and with a kind voice.

"I asked him," "to tell me where the boys were standing at when the gunfire started?"

Peyton told me again that two of them was standing against that wall over there and the other two was on the other side of the bank.

So I said, they were two of them standing on the left side of the bank and two was standing on the right side of the bank.

"Is that right Peyton?"

He said, yes.

"How is that even possible, when your workstation is in the very back of the bank, beside the bank volt?"

I am missing something the Sheriff said. You said that they were four of them that come into the bank and two of them had gone back outside to stand with the horses. Now in my books that make's about four of them in all. Peyton, you said that they were more that the first time that you told me the tale.

Peyton was so nerves that he didn't even catch on to what the Sheriff had said to him. "What did they do then, the Sheriff ask?

Peyton told him that they pulled their guns and said, that this was a "bank robbery" and I was to get the money and the land deeds and put them in a bag and give it to them, so I did. I put everything that was in the bank vault into one of the bank bags and I took it to them and that's when one of them shot me.

"The Sheriff asked Peyton," "how was that even possible when they were standing over here by the door?"

Peyton looked around the bank really fast and then he changed his story. He then said, that one of them had come over to where he was working. He told me that this was a bank heist and he wanted all the money put into this bag that he had with him. And if I didn't do this, he would shoot me and take the money and the land deeds himself. He said that the money didn't belong to me, so it wasn't worth him dying over. I did as they asked and they still shot me.

"The Sheriff" "asked Payton" "if they shot him first or did they shoot the two in the face first?"

Payton was quite for a second or two and then he answered the Sheriff and said, that they killed those two men and then they shoot me.

The Sheriff told him that something was wrong with his story and he knew that he must have been involved somehow in this bank heist, because if they wanted him dead, he would be dead. Besides Peyton your account of how many men there was really is off by two somehow.

Peyton just stood there, with this blank look on his face. He knew what he had already told them was a lie and he knew that the Sheriff was on to him.

It's hard for me to remember Payton told us. It all happened so fast and he must have told us wrong. He said, let me start over, so the Sheriff and I knew right then and there that Peyton was not telling the whole truth.

The Sheriff said, well then Peyton, take a deep breath and start from the beginning one more time. This time, the Sheriff said, think about it for a second and then tell us again, your side of the story.

Peyton wiped the sweat from his forehead and he started again.

He said that he was done waiting on some people and they had left. That's when they come into the bank and they walked around in here for a few minutes and then two of them went on that side of the bank and one of them went on the other side and one came back to where I was working.

Yes, that's right he "meant to say to his self" because he cough himself talking out loud and he stopped and looked up at me and he knew that he was busted.

I told him that the Sheriff and I both knew, that he had something to do with the heist and the best thing, he could do now, was tell the truth. He started to cry a little bit and I put my hand up on his shoulder and then I hugged him. This calmed him down somewhat and then he told us the truth.

He said, that he had been part of the heist all along and that he had already put the deeds into one of the bags and then he put the money into another. When they got there, they made it look as if it was a real bank heist. They grabbed the bag that I gave to them and I had already hidden the bag with the money in it before they got there. He said that they were supposed to shot me so no one would think that he had any part to do with the heist. They were just supposed to wound me in the shoulder, just to make it look as if it was a robbery gone badly. They shot me in the shoulder and then they was supposed to leave but they turned and shot the other two in the face. They were not supposed to shot them.

I don't know why they did that, so don't ask me anything about it. They told me that no one else was supposed to get hurt but they lied. The deeds were all that they really wanted so they could buy the land holders out and they planned on reselling the land to the Rail Road. They were planning on getting rich because of the Rail Road would be buying up all the land from them. They could sell it for five times what they had paid for it, to start with. I knew that I was supposed to get a part of that money also whenever they resold the land to the railroad. When they shot the other two like they did, I knew that they would kill me too, as soon as they could, just to keep me from talking.

"The Sheriff asked him," "who was the other two men that they had shot?"

Peyton told us that he first met them in New York and they wouldn't tell him what their names was. So he had no idea who they really were. I was the only one that was supposed to get hurt, just wounded a little bit, not those other two. I hid the money because I knew that they were here just for the deeds and my wife was with child and we needed the money for the baby.

"What happen to the real plan," "I do not know, but this time," "I told you the real truth now?"

I am so sorry and I wished that I didn't have any part in it but I did, for that I am so sorry.

I walk over to him and I hugged him and I told him that the Sheriff and I might have some more questions for him later on.

The Sheriff walked over to him and took him by his good arm and took him to jail. He locked him up with Sam.

Some people in town saw what was happening and they ran to find out why the Sheriff had arrested Peyton but he told them that he couldn't tell them because it was an ongoing case. He would tell everybody at the right time and not before then. There would be some more arrest that he was planning to make in this case.

Well, Hazel the Sheriff said, I do believe that we have answered our first questions.

I told him that he was right. We now know that the bank teller was not only in on the heist but he was the one that told them where the land deeds were being held at. He also told them, when and where to rob the bank. They all had set out to make it look as if it was supposed to be a real bank robbery, which had gone wrong. That was their intent all along. That's why they picked our bank to rob because Peyton had told them, when and where. We also know that the talk of the Rail Road must have some sort of truth about it coming to Maple Wood. They say that money is the root of all evil.

In this case, I say they are right, yes Hazel the Sheriff said to her. We also know why the teller was shot but not killed like the other two was. We need to find the other five that was involved with this pretend heist.

Well, Miss Hazel, we will have to wait until tomorrow to answer some more of the questions so we might as well go to bed and start out fresh tomorrow. I am tired aren't you, my dear. Hazel said that she was tired also, so they called it a night.

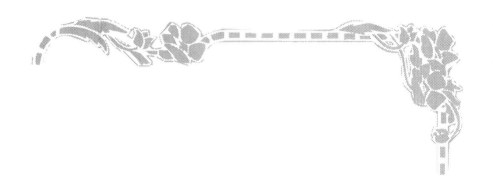

CHAPTER THREE

HAZEL AND THE SHERIFF'S NEW LIFE TOGETHER JUST A FEW MORE QUESTIONS TO ASK!

It's a whole new day Hazel thought to herself as she jumped up out of her bed and started to get ready to greet the brand new day. After she was ready, she walked over to the Sheriff's side of the bed and she took one of her guns out and for kicks, she fired it out the window that was beside the bed.

The Sheriff jumped straight up in bed and she squalled out really fast, go get them, Sheriff. He ran straight from the end of the bed and fell flat onto the floor. He had busted his nose whenever he hit the floor with his face.

I all most felt sorry for him but face it, that's not who I really am.
I couldn't help but to laugh at him, though. He, on the other hand,
didn't see the humor in it, for some reason. He yelled at me and said
that was not funny at all Hazel and you know it. He was pissed by this
time and that made me feel better. It's about time that the old man got
his temper up, she thought to herself.

I took off running down the stairs as he ran after me. There at the
bottom of the stairs there stood James our mayor and about four or five
other people. There was nothing wrong with that I guessed expect when
the Sheriff came running after me, for what I had done, he forgot one
thing. He didn't put his tracers on and he was still in his night clothes as
he made his way down the stairs to where all the people were standing.
He was now really mad, by this point.

He snapped at the people and asked them what they were all doing
there in the diner that time of the morning.

James said that they were worried about him.

He said, what the "hell for."

The Mayor James said that they heard gunfire and they thought
that Hazel had finally killed you off, for good this time.

The Sheriff looked at me and I had my hand covering my mouth,
trying not to laugh but I was never too good at hiding the obvious.

He wanted my head on a platter and I knew it, all too well. He was so hot that he was steaming. He just turned and stomped his way back up the stairs and we all just couldn't hold it in no more.

I swear that you could hear us laughing so loud, that they must have heard us plum over into the next town. You know, I might have taken this floor plaything, just a little bit too far this time! "Nan"!

After the Sheriff cool his self off and, this time, I was the one that had to play nice to get back on his good side again. Yes, that's right, I said, I played nice but don't mistake it for, "I said that I sorry." There isn't a man in the world that I am willing to say that to, not even the man that I married. Maybe one day but that day isn't this one.

I thought that I would be nice and go see how Payton's wife was doing since the Sheriff and I put him in jail yesterday. Payton said that she was with child and all that I could think about was that she must be really stressed out by all of this. I went to her house and she was just arriving back home herself. Now that struck me as really odd. If she was from New York and only been here for two years, where in the world could she had been coming from this early in the morning, I thought to myself. I knew that she had not been to see her husband because she was coming back into town and the Jailhouse was in the other direction. She was there in front of her house as I arrived. I walked up to her and introduced myself and I told her my name was Hazel.

Jamie said that she already knew who I was, from the Diner.

I said that I wanted to talk to her about what had happened with her husband yesterday.

She turned her head really fast and looked at me and said.

"What was I talking about?"

That question threw up a red flag to start with, right off the bat. Now I know that I am not really a lady, to hear some people say but I do know where my husband is at all the time. She, on the other hand, had no idea that her husband was in jail. So I sat her down and I told her everything that had happened.

Jamie told me that she was out of town for a few days and that she had just gotten back when I showed up.

I thought that sounded a little funny, but I gave her the benefit of the doubt. I keep on telling her about what had happened to her man and when I got done telling her. Jamie seemed to either not care or she had lied when she said that she was out of town. There was something fishy going on here I thought to myself. She was hiding something, as sure as I was sitting there on her front porch. She was not sad nor was she even worried or if she were, I sure couldn't tell it. She struck me, as to be the coldest one women that I had ever met. There was no feeling of remorse or nothing coming from her. She didn't have a clue as to who, she was actually talking to.

I am the type of person, that likes to ask questions and when I do, I expect someone to have an answer to that question, which I had asked.

I knew that she look familiar to me but I just couldn't place where I have seen her before. I am telling you that I know her from somewhere. Then it came to me where I knew her. I had to make sure to see if I was right, though.

I started questioning her about New York. I told her about, what her man had said, about where he had met her, there in New York. I told her that he said, that she had to sweep him off of his feet, the first time that he saw her. He was in love at first sight, he told me.

"I ask her" "if she felt the same way about him?"

She just simply said yes, nothing more than that or nothing less either, than that. Short and sweet, just like her man's answers was. I had this feeling in the bottom of my stomach that she was lying about something and I was determined to find out what.

"I asked Jamie" "if it was true that you could see everything that you would ever want to see, there on that place called, Time Square?"

Jamie said yes, they have everything there that you could ever want.

Jamie was like her husband. She answered me with short responses and keep to the point. She was hiding something and this old bloodhound was done after the rabbit's tail and there was no way to call me off the scent, even if you tried. She was more than likely, never in New York in her lifetime. She was however taught by the same person how to lie, which had taught her husband, Peyton. We all know where that ended him up at.

Somehow she was connected to the bank robbery and I was going to prove it or die to try. Sense I was not planning on dying today, she was all mine and by this time, I was all over her and she knew it.

I tore back into her and New York. I started asking her more and more questions about New York and she, kelp trying to change the subject.

"When was the last time that you were in Water Town," "there just off Time Square" "there in New York City," "I ask her?"

Jamie said that was where she done all of her best shopping at.

That is when I let her know that I knew that she was lying about New York City.

Jamie said that I didn't know what I was talking about.

I told her that Water Town is a place that was about twenty miles outside of New York City and not nowhere near Time Square.

Jamie knew that I was on to her and I also knew that she was indeed lying. I told her where I knew her from, and it was not New York City.

"You are from around here aren't you," "I ask her?"

Jamie just looked at me, while not saying a word. Jamie knew that she was busted and I was the one that busted her.

"I said" "that you are old man Donald's child," "aren't you?"

Jamie just nodded her head at me and then she said, that she was his daughter and she had been raised out West by her Mother. Her dad wanted the land, so he could sell it and get himself out of debt.

That would answer the question of who would want the land deeds.

She told me that her father had been selling off all of his cattle and trying to raise the money up to buy out the other landholders just so he could sell the land back to the Railroad Company.

That means that Donald was behind all of this.

Jamie told me that her father was really deep into debt and he was about to lose everything that he had worked so hard for. All that he needed was to find out who owned what land and how much they still owed the bank for it. That was the only way that he could think of, to raise enough money to do it with.

That means that all this was done just because of the greed of one man.

I told her that I knew and understood why he would want to do such a thing but it was still wrong.

"I ask her" "if she knew that two of his hired hands died in that bank robbery?"

Jamie just broke down and started to cry when I told her that. She had no idea that they had been two men that had died there.

Jamie said that her daddy never told her that when she had talked to him last night. He said that everything had gone, just as he had wanted it to.

Peyton was the one that told him where the land deeds were and when it would be a good time to rob the bank. Jamie had proved that her husband Peyton was the inside man all along.

"I ask her, what he had meant when he said that to her?"

Jamie said that she had no idea what the plan really was because her daddy never told her the real plan and what was actually supposed to happen. She didn't even know that her husband had been caught. He was not supposed to get hurt but they shot him anyhow.

When Jamie told me that, I knew that she had not been out of town as she had said but she had been out to her father's place instead.

Daddy said that they had to shoot him to keep anyone from finding out that he was in on it the whole time. He was mad because they were just supposed to wing Peyton, not actually shoot him.

That explains the reason why the other two men were shot in the face. They all just did it because they wanted to, not because Donald had told them to.

I told her that they had shot those other two, in the face so we couldn't find out who they really were. This all had to be planned out by someone. They just didn't shot them for no reason. I am pissed because one of them so called bank robbers shot out my picture windows in my dinner.

I need for you to tell me the whole truth Jamie and do not lie to me because I will find out if you do and I will be very mad at you, not your father.

She said that she had told me the truth and she didn't know nothing else about her father's plan.

"I ask her" "if Payton had told the truth when he said that you are with child?"

Jamie put her head down and she said that she wasn't. That was how her father got him to go along with the plan. He told me to tell Peyton that I was with child and I was to tell him that we would need a lot more money for the baby. We would need a lot more than what we had saved up. That is when he decided to go along with daddy's plan. He didn't want to, but my father and I talked him into it. He got drug into this whole mess because of a lie.

"Peyton didn't know that those men were going to shot the others two in the face like that did he" "I ask Jamie?"

She said, as far as she knew no and neither did her father. That is why Daddy was so mad when he found out the truth. They first told Daddy that they had gotten shot while trying to rob the bank. He didn't find out until later that they had killed them because they didn't want to share the money that Daddy was going to pay them for doing that job they had done for him.

Peyton was so happy when I told him that I was with child. He had so many plans for the three of us and what he had a plan for our futures. He wanted me and the baby to move out west to where my Mother was at, so she could help me with the baby. He wasn't thinking of himself but of the baby and me. I never meant someone that put my needs before theirs in my lifetime. That's why I loved him so much.

I also love my father and that's why I agreed to talk Peyton into all of this. I guess I am to blame as much as my father is for all of this.

"I asked her," "where her father was right now?"

She said that he was out to his ranch or at least that is where I left him at the last time that I saw him.

"Where are the other four men that robbed the bank with your husband?"

She said that they were more than likely with her father. He had a lot of people that work for him. I don't know who those other four men really were because my father never did tell me. It could have been any of them, as far as I knew. I don't really want to know who they were.

I am so sorry for all of this and Peyton was innocence. He just did what he did, because I asked him to do it. He would do anything for me and I used that against him. That makes me to be just as evil as my father is, in my books doesn't it Hazel.

I told her pretty much so!

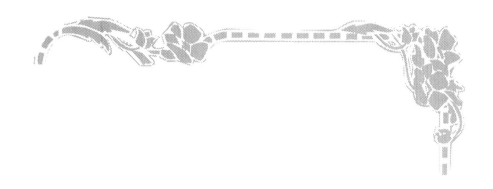

CHAPTER FOUR

THE TAKE DOWN

Hazel had finished with her talk with Peyton's wife Jamie and she walked her over to the Sheriff's office there at the Jailhouse. The Sheriff locked her up with her husband and Sam.

I told the Sheriff everything that we had talked about. I now had some answers to the questions that we had.

Now all that we have left to do was come up with a plan to trap all of them, hopefully at the same time. That would be nice but it doesn't always work out like that and I should know that better than anyone. The Sheriff and I put a plan together and we knew that we would run into some kind of trouble, so we gather up twenty other men and we all headed out to Mr. Donald Macqueen's place.

Donald was the worse type of man. He thought that just because he had a lot of money that meant, that he would always be above the law. This made him very dangerous indeed. He thought that he was untouchable. He must have thought of himself as some sort of a God among men.

After the Sheriff and I told them what kind of a person that, we was going up against. The Sheriff had made them all deputies and now they had no other choice but to enforce the law. They felt better about themselves in case they had to take another man's life.

That in itself takes a great toll on your soul, regardless of how hard that you try to keep from it. After a while, if you were unable to turn away from all the killing. You would become so cold hearted. They say that you just forget how to feel after you kill so many others, that's when you lose yourself. That little tin star gave the men a much-needed boost in their confidence department but it would not save their lives.

We were now ready for whatever that Mr. Donald Macqueen had planned for us. There is no telling what we are in for and the Sheriff told the men that were with us, to be careful. I don't want no one to think that you are going out there to be some kind of a hero. That kind of thinking will do nothing but get you killed. They all said that they would listen to the Sheriff's every word and they all understood what he was trying to say to them.

We made it to the ranch and sure enough, we road right into gunfire at the front gates. He had guards posted all along the gates and fences that were in front of his ranch. Donald must have been planning this whole thing from the start. He knew that he would be caught and this must be his plan on getting out of it. There was more to this and the Sheriff and I knew it.

There was one of them shot dead right off the bat, just as soon as they started to open fire upon us and as we were returning their fire. That's when one of them was hit. We back them up towards the barn were the painted horse was at, with our gunfire, the first time that the Sheriff and I were out there.

The horse was not there now. All the horses were now gone and I say that the men that we were looking for, that robbed the bank was long gone by know along with the horses.

We had them badly outnumbered but they still wouldn't let us get no closer to the house. The house set back behind the barn. They had our men pin down there by the stables.

What was Donald's real intentions, I couldn't help but to wonder to myself.

The Sheriff and I took about four other men with us and we snuck around to the side of the barn, and we made our way towards the main house. The other boys were left there at the barn to keep their attention away from what we were trying to do.

When we had made it to the main house, sure enough, he had men there also. That just goes to show you what money will buy.

Jamie was right when she said that, her father had a lot of people that work for him. I felt as if we was up against an army.

One by one, they fell to the waste side, as we keep getting closer to the main house.

But, this didn't seem to bother them for some strange reason.

I could see about four or five of them still standing there on the front porch. Mr. Donald Macqueen wasn't one of them. He must have lost the will to take someone else's life or he just didn't have the guts to do it himself.

Where could he be I thought to myself as the gunfire keep on, for a while. They were dead or half dead body's laying just about, anywhere and everywhere you looked. They had lost so many of their men and we had lost some as well but we couldn't stop now. We were too close to the main house to quit.

So much innocence blood lost for nothing other one man's greed for money I thought to myself, as the gunfire just keep on going from both sides. I knew that Mr. Donald had to be hold up inside of the house because there wasn't nowhere else he could be hiding at or, at least, I could tell. They were guarding it too hard for him not to be in there. For a moment, I thought that the gunfire was coming to an end.

Then out of nowhere, a lot of people poured out of the main house onto the front porch. They were now women and young children that they had lined the entire front porch with.

"What kind of a man would put those women and children in harm's way like that?"

He was using them as a human shield against us. Now that goes to show you what kind of a man Mr. Donald Macqueen really was.

The Sheriff yelled out for all of us to stop firing. He didn't want no one to die, that didn't have to. Do not shoot at the women or the children, he said.

What we didn't know was that Donald had given guns to them and told them to shoot at us. He was trying to confuse us for some reason or another.

"Donald had a plan but what was it" "I asked the Sheriff?"

He said that he didn't know but what else could we do but keep on fighting.

Donald wanted us to stay right where we were for some reason. He knew that none of us was willing to shoot at the women or children. He was smarter than what I thought.

The men that he had hired to fight this battle for him, that was still standing, ran right past the women and the children, back inside of the house.

They left all of those women and children there on the front porch. He was using them as some sort of a sacrifice. Donald didn't care if they lived or died. They didn't mean nothing to him or his hired hands. He knew that we wouldn't fire upon the women and none of us wanted to be responsible for shooting, one of those innocence children.

They didn't have nothing to do with this mess. They were shooting, just to be shooting. They were not trying to shoot at us. They were just firing into the wind, without having any target in their minds. They just wanted to keep us pinned down but for what reason.

"What was Donald's actually planning on doing," "I wondered," "so I ask the Sheriff?"

I don't really know the Sheriff said, but he had went and done it know. He had really pissed me off by using those families to fight his battles for him.

What kind of monster would use women and children to fight his battle for him, I asked the Sheriff?

I don't really know but he has planned this whole thing out. He is the worst kind of outlaw I am afraid to say. The kind that has a death wish and does not care who gets hurt.

We just have to be smarter than he is Hazel. Right now he thinks he's winning. "Hell Hazel" right now he is winning the Sheriff said. Let's all calm down and not lose our heads and hurt any of them.

Sheriff you and I will make our way to the back of the house and see what he is hiding back there. The rest of you boys stay here and keep their attention on you all, so they want to see what the Sheriff and I are trying doing.

Keep your head down and flow me Sheriff and we will make our way out back Hazel told him.

We stayed as close to the ground as we possibly could have. We made it to where we could see the back of the house and there were some women and children there on the back porch also. Donald was sure guarding that house carefully for some reason.

He had it locked down tighter than Fort Knocks. There was something that he was guarding inside of that house and I don't think that it was himself. Out in the back yard was nothing but what looked like an outside toilet. That struck me as being odd.

What would a man with that kind of a set up and money, have an outside toilet in the back yard, I said to the Sheriff.

We will take a look at it the Sheriff said when all of this is over with.

Then something happened, that none of us will ever forget, to the day that we die.

That big house that was so heavily guarded, by so many women and children, exploded into a ball of fire.

The noise from that blast was indescribable. The house went up into a ball of fire, taking all of those innocence women and children with it.

All of the Sheriff's men and myself was left with after the house exploded was, that now we were covered with all their blood and leftover guts. As the Sheriff and all of his men stood there while covered with the aftermath of what had just happened.

Some of them just started throwing up everything that they had in their stomachs. We were amazed at what just happened. He killed everybody that was even anywhere near that house. Then if that wasn't bad enough, the barn went up in another ball of fire a few minutes later, just like the main house did. There wasn't nothing left but busted planks and people crying as the smoke cleared. The only building that didn't explode was that little outhouse in the back yard.

"What just happened here," "I asked the Sheriff?"

He said that Donald must have blew the whole thing up including himself. He rather take himself out his own way, instead of letting us take him out.

There was so many life's that he had taken to hell with him for no reason, I said, to the Sheriff.

All of our men that was still standing put their guns away and started to help as many women and children as they could. None of us will ever forget this day. I sent two of the boy's back to town to get as many people as they could find to help us with the cleanup. The worst thing about this whole thing was the great number of lives that was lost on account of Donald Macqueen just was determined to get by with his part in all of this.

It was indescribable what my eyes was seeing. I didn't want to look at those small children just lying there torn to shreds but I was left without any choice. They need my help now, as well as everybody else's help that we could get. There was no reason for all this bloodshed that happen here today.

The survivors were all women and small children. They had burns and missing body parts. The ones that did survived the blast had lost all their love one's in it. They all wished that they too had not survived the explosion, as we recovered their loved one's bodies from the fire. So much destruction and lost souls.

"How can one man do all of this," "I asked you?"

There is no answer to what had to happen here today, that I can give to you, other than its man's way or no way!

We all work way up into the night, recovering bodies, both dead and alive. The mess went on for two days. The lost body count was now over, one hundred.

As for the outside toilet that was out back of the main house. It was for those women and young children to us.

When we had removed all the bodies from the house and the barn, I noticed something. Donald nor his hired hands were in the mess that was left behind, in the blast from the house. There were about ten men there at the barn but none of them from where the house once stood. They were all most all women and children.

"Where were all the men at," "I ask the Sheriff?"

"How did he pull this off I wonder to myself and I told the Sheriff what I had found out?"

The Sheriff and I set out to get some answers from the only people that was left to ask. The women.

The Sheriff and I, both agreed and we set out to find out what had actually happened to Donald and his hired hands. We had done found out that the women and the children were brought there by Donald and his men to work on his ranch. He was using them as slave labor. That's why they were so many of them.

Donald had told them, when he gave those guns to them, that if they didn't defend the house, that he would shoot them also. They didn't have any choice but to shoot or die the women told us. Either way, they were going to still die either by Donald's hand or us. Their lives were now over with as far as they were concerned.

The women, on the other hand, didn't plan on hurting any of us. They had done lost too much already. They had come up with a plan of their own.

They had told everyone not to shoot at us but they would instead, just fire their weapons, over the top of our heads. They said that they didn't have no problem with us. So they really didn't want to shoot any of us, for no reason other than he told them to do so.

They had done what they did, just because they were forced into it. This was not their fight but Donald's.

The Sheriff and I told them, that we had thought the same thing and that none of the survivors will be charged with any crimes. As far as we were concerned you all have lost enough at the hand of that man.

We were still looking for Donald and his hired hands. The women had said, that he had made the men dig a tunnel under the main house and he wanted it to come out on the other side of the barn.

That was what that snake was hiding. He had a way out of there and he just didn't want us to see him leaving. This man had planned it all out in advance.

The women said, when the tunnel that he made the men dig was finished, he shoot all the men that had worked on that tunnel for him. They lost all their husbands and young men that day.

He had them dig a big hole in the ground, just passed the barn. When they got done with it, they lined all the men that were left and all the young boys up that had worked on that tunnel and shot them and threw their dead bodies into that whole.

Donald was afraid that they would tell on him if he left them alive. A dead man can tell no tells.

We had to bury all of our loved one's in that big grave. I know that that sounded as if that was the hardest thing that we had to do that day but the waiting was the hardest for us. It came after we buried our loved one's dead bodies.

"I ask one of them," "what they meant by saying that?"

One of the women just said to the Sheriff and myself, we was waiting for our turn to die. "That sounds cold but at least in death, it would be over with!"

That snake had them dig an escape tunnel for him and his men. That means that Donald and his men didn't die in that blast. They couldn't have, they were already gone when the house exploded.

I didn't know how a man like that could live with what he had done, but I was, even more, determined than ever now, to get him for what he had done to all those families, I told the Sheriff.

We had gone back to the barn and sure enough, we found that tunnel that the women had told us about. We traced it from the house, all the way, to the other side of the barn. There were a lot of horse tracks there and we know now what way they were heading. They were going to try to get away from us by going over the Mountain top and into Canada.

Donald might have thought that he had beat us but he don't know who he was dealing with. The Sheriff and I were going to make him pay for what he had done, one way or another that man and his hired hands will pay dearly for what they had done here.

That much the Sheriff and I promise you!

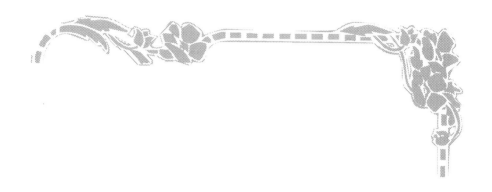

CHAPTER FIVE

THE POSSE IS OUT FOR BLOOD

We were now in a rush to catch Donald Macqueen and his men before they could reach the top of the Mountain. From there they stood an excellent chance of getting away from us. From there they only had to step one foot onto the other side of the Mountain top and they would be in Canada. The Sheriff couldn't touch them there. They could go just about anywhere they wanted to and we would never see them again. That was their plan all along and it was now up to us to stop them.

The winter snows don't melt as fast on top of the Mountains as it does down here in the lower valleys. It stays on the upper part of the Mountain tops just about year round. They couldn't run far and broad enough to get away from us for the crimes against humanity that they were guilty of. We would find him regardless of what rock that snake crawls up under. There was no way that he was going to live life as a free man when he had killed so many and destroyed so many lives, just to do it.

He had left his Ranch and his daughter as well and his daughters husband, Peyton. Jamie said that his wife was out west, so he didn't have any family left. He just didn't care that much was for sure. This man was out for nobody but his self.

We sure didn't have any trouble finding enough men in our town, to form a Posse. All that we had to do was put out the word, which the Sheriff and I were going after Donald and his men.

I went over to the Jailhouse to speak to Jamie, Donald's daughter. I told her what had happened there at her father's Ranch. She was in tears and so was Payton. Even Sam had tears in his eyes as I told them all what had happened at Donald's Ranch.

The Sheriff came over to the Jailhouse to get me and he walked over to Sam Jail Cell door and he took the key off the wall and opened his cell door.

The Sheriff looked right into Sam's eyes and said, that he was giving him a chance to clear his name. He then turned and looked at Peyton and told him the same thing. The Sheriff said that he needed every man that he could get, to go after Donald and his men.

The Sheriff said, that if they wanted their freedom back, now was the time to ask for it.

They looked at each other only for a second and both of them said that they would be more than glad to help bring them all to justice.

The Sheriff then gave them their guns back to each of them. They strapped them on as they made their way to the door.

The Sheriff said, boys if I have any trouble out of either one of you. Make no mistake, I will shoot you both dead, where you stand. They agreed with everything that the Sheriff said.

There were about forty men and myself going after them. I asked Jamie if she wanted to help by telling us anything that she might know where her father might be heading for.

She told me that, they had this hunting cabin, which they all went to every year.

She also said, that was the only place that she knew, that he would go. Jamie said that it was where they spend a lot of time at when she was growing up. If there were any place in the world that he would run to, it would be there. What makes me think that is where they have gone to, is because of the cabins location. It sets out to its self in a deep valley. There is nothing around for miles.

I told Jamie that he has been gone for almost three days now and they didn't have any time more to waste. If they were going to get them, they would have to do it now.

She said that she was the only one that knew the right pass to take in the Mountains. "Jamie ask" "if she could come and show us the right way?"

"I asked her" "if she was willing to help put her own father into Jail?"

Jamie told me that she stop seeing him as her father and now she only knew him for the monster that he really was. My mother said that she couldn't stay married to him because she thought that there was no curlier man on this earth. I guess she was right. I only wished that I would have listened to her now.

I told her that he would go to Jail for the rest of his life for what he had done. He has given our town a black stain, which would leave us all with our heads hung low and we all will have to live with that mark forever.

Jamie said, that the man she loved and knew as her father was long gone by now. She would not have no problem with watching him receiving justice for killing all those people.

I took the keys that the Sheriff had hung back up on the wall and I set her free. Now there would be two women going on this trip.

When I took her outside to where the posse was waiting. They wanted to hang her right then and there for what her father had done. I told the crowd that, she was not her father and they would not touch her for his crimes. That right belongs to her father, not her father's daughter.

I told them that she was not her father and she was the only one that knew where he had gone to. She was now under my protection and she was not to be harmed. I repeated what I just had said and this time, I told them that if any of them, touch her that I would shoot them dead. They all knew that I meant business. They all shut up and we got up on our horses and we were all off.

Jamie said that it takes about four days to get to the cabin from here but if we ride hard, we will make it in two days or maybe three. Jamie said that the trick to finding the cabin was in taking the right pass, at the top of the Mountain.

If you took the wrong pass there on top of the Mountain, you would be lost in the snow covered Mountains peaks forever. There you would have to deal with snow and hunger, not to say anything about freezing to death. For the lucky ones, an avalanche of snow from one of the high peaks will take you out quickly. That is the easy way out but it will be a quick death and you wouldn't suffer, too much.

We rode harder than any of us had ever rode before. The Mountain was steep and the trails were narrow but even that didn't slow us down. We were working like a well-oiled machine. They were all looking out for each other and that made us all feel like one big family.

After all, we all live there in the same town and we had to clean up our own mess. We had rode throughout the night and the whole next day when the horses were about to give out and fall dead right underneath of us. We had no other choice but to stop and let our horses rest.

The men were what I was worried about when it came to Jamie and her husband Peyton's wellbeing. I had my eyes on them and so did the Sheriff.

Jamie had helped me cook for all the men and as she feed each one of them. Jamie said that she was so sorry for what she had done and for what her husband Peyton had done. She told them all that, she knew that her family had done so much harm to our town and she hoped that they could find it in their hearts to forgive them for their part in all of this.

They all said that they knew that she and Peyton had nothing to do with what had happened, there at her father ranch. They never said much and you could tell that she was hurt by their actions but there was nothing that she was going to do to change their minds. She could only do the right thing now and worry about the rest later on.

I walked over to her and hugged her and said, that everything always seems to work its self out. Things like this have to run it's on course. Just keep on trying, that's all that you can really do for now. "I asked her while we were doing the dishes," "what was she going to do about Peyton?"

She said that she told him everything that she told me and she could only ask him for his forgiveness.

"I asked her," "what did he say when she told him about the baby?"

He has never spoke another word to me since I told him that I was never with child.

"I ask her" "if he has even spoken to her while they both was locked up in Jail together?"

He didn't say a word. He just sat there and cried. With him not saying a word to me, hurt me almost as much as it did, when I first told him, that I was with child. I was only doing what my father had told me to do. Peyton only did, what I ask him to do. We were both used by my father. I just hope that I can make it up to him somehow because I do love him so much.

"I ask her" "if she told him that?"

She said that was hard for her to do, especially when he would not even look her in the eye.

I told her not to give up on him yet, he still might come around. I think that he still loves you and things may change when this is all over with.

After we had all rested for about four hours. I told them all to mount up and followed Jamie and the Sheriff and myself.

Jamie said that the pass was just up ahead and for us all to be very quiet as we enter the pass because any loud noise could cause an avalanche. The snow would come down and if it didn't kill us right off, it would trap us in the valley where the cabin is until the snow melts next spring. That's why I think that my father and his men are there.

They might have already blown the snow pack down, to cover his trail. When we all made it to the pass and it sure wasn't easy but we made it.

I told them all to follow my horse's tracks and not to say a word. Walk your horses in single file and be as quiet as possible. We started going through the pass in single file, right behind each other. The snow was piled up on the top of the Mountain and it was a scary sight indeed, just to look at but we all made it through the pass without any trouble.

Once we all made it through and we were safely on the other side of the Mountain. Jamie told us that the cabin was just below the snow melt. The Sheriff and I took the lead and we rode the horses down the Mountain and we were just at the bottom of the snowfall when the Sheriff saw signs of other horses had been through there. We would have never found this spot if it hadn't been for Jamie's help.

She told us that the cabin was stuck back into the next valley. She said that it was back all the way up to the cliffs. There was but only one way in or out, from where the cabin sets. If I know my father, he will have guards posted at the mouth of the valley.

The Sheriff said, for her to just point him in the right direction and leave the rest up to him and Hazel. We will take it from here the Sheriff told Jamie. We rode the horses up to the valley entrance and the Sheriff and I went on by ourselves.

The Sheriff told the others to keep as quiet as they could and for them to come as soon as they heard gunfire. The Sheriff knew that if one gun went off, then they would know that we were on to them. The Sheriff and I left our horses and we went from there on foot. When we got within sight of the valley, sure enough, about four men were guarding the entrance to the cabin.

The Sheriff and I were as we work as one mind since we had been to gather for so long. I knew what he was going to do, even before he did it and he knew what I was going to do. The Sheriff and I made our way to where we were right below them. They didn't even see us coming. They thought that they were well hidden there in that valley, free and protected from the law. To them, they had it made.

The Sheriff had brought his bow and arrow with him and he planned on killing them with it because they would not see an arrow coming at them until it was too late. His Indian brother Silver Cloud had taught him how to hunt and how to shoot the bow. He told me to wait until I heard from him. He said that I may need you to kill one or two of them if they see me.

I liked the gun and I was the best shot in town. If I fired my weapon, I always hit my target. The Sheriff went around the mountain side as if he was a snake. He had this way about him whenever he was on the hunt, to where he hunted like a snake would. He would lay still and when they came into striking range, he would strike. He never missed his target. I still don't know how he makes his body so low to the ground but that's their Indians way. They taught him how to get as low to the ground as if he was a snake himself.

He pulled the bow back and he rolled over onto his back and he let the first arrow lose. It hit its target. He had hit the first man in the face. The arrow had gone through the bottom of his jaw and right out the top of his head. He couldn't say nothing because the Sheriff had pinned his mouth closed with that arrow. The only noise that he made was when he hit the ground dead.

Then the Sheriff crept along the ground as he got a little closer to the next man. When the Sheriff got him in his cross hairs, he shot another arrow at him. He hit him in the neck, cutting his throat with that arrow.

He took aim at the third man as he came over to see what had happened to the other two. And the Sheriff took him out with one shot to the chest. Blood poured out of his mouth as the arrow the Sheriff had hit him with, went straight through his heart.

The next man saw what was happening and he tried to make a run for it when the Sheriff took another shot and he hit him in the back. He fell face forward onto the ground.

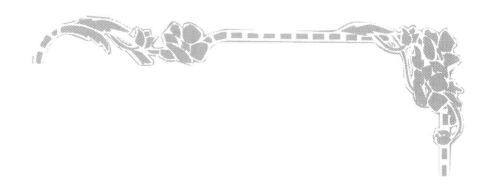

CHAPTER SIX

THE CONFESSION

The cost was now cleared thanks to the Sheriff and his ability to use the bow and arrow so well. The only lives that were lost were the bad guys.

I made my way up to where the Sheriff was at and he told me to stay back as he crawled up a little closer to the front of the cabin.

I told him that I would watch out for his back as he made his way to the front of the cabin.

The Sheriff once more got as low to the ground as he could have and he started making his way closer to where they were. He had made it up to where they had their horses at. He opened the gates and set their horses lose and then he hid as the horses ran free.

When they heard their horses running, lose. They poured out of that cabin as if it was a big hornet's nest, just full of hornets and they were for sure mad.

The Sheriff was well hidden as they started to run after their horses. He had set them up in a trap so he could get them to separate from each other. He used the horses to do that. They were paying more attention to the loose horses running free than they were to the real reason why they were loose to start with.

The Sheriff had taken out about five more of them before they knew what was happening. He ran out of arrows and he started using his guns.

That was the sign that we were all waiting for.

Our men came at them from every direction. They didn't know what way to aim their guns at as our men picked them off two by two. There was a few that had made it back inside of the cabin and now it become a standoff. We had to wait them out now. They had given us enough time though to get all of our people into position.

We were not going to waste our time here and now on this, the Sheriff said. This is not going to be one of those standoff's that last for days and they always end up with the same resort. You don't know if he is planning on blowing that cabin up just as he did, down in the valley at his Ranch.

The Sheriff sent for Jamie and her husband Peyton, to come and see if they could talk her father into given himself up.

Jamie told the Sheriff that she would do anything that he wanted her to do. She said that she would try her best to talk him into standing down.

Jamie walked up as close to the cabin as she possibly could have, without getting shot herself. She had gotten in place and Peyton was there by her side.

We still didn't know if Donald was even there. No one had seen him or heard anything from his men to his where a bout's.

When Jamie started yelling towards the cabin for her father to answer her.

There was nothing at first but a man like Donald couldn't stay quiet for long. He liked to call the shots. He had this big ego and that was what the Sheriff and I were counting own. If he was in that cabin, he would answer his daughter back. Sure enough, he answered her call out to him.

He said that for us to go away.

Like that was ever going to happen.

If we didn't do as he said, then he would blow the cabin up, just like he did the house and the barn. He told us that if he left the Mountain top today, he was more than willing to be dead when he did it.

That was all the Sheriff needed to hear. The sheriff knew that he was planning on us killing him and his men, so he would never give up regardless of how long we waited for.

He told the men to open fire upon the cabin and they all did just as the Sheriff had told them all to do so.

They filled the whole valley full of the sound of gunfire. They were shooting the cabin with everything that they had. It went on for some time before the Sheriff told them to stop and let Jamie and Peyton try again, to get them to stand down.

The cabin had more lead in it by this time than most boats had.

Jamie tried once more but nothing happened. They still yelled out that they would rather be dead than give up.

The Sheriff told one of our boys to go and get the arrows back from the boys that he had shot with them, earlier.

"I ask the Sheriff," "what was he planning on doing?"

The Sheriff said that a man like that has but only one thing on his mind. That is a death wish. The only way to handle him was going to be by burning them out of there.

The bullets would not go through the logs that the cabin was made of so we will burn them out. The boys went and retrieved the arrows from the dead bodies and brought them back to the Sheriff.

The only thing between us and that cabin was two big oak trees. They were huge and the limbs that were on the trees keep us from getting closer than what we already were.

The Sheriff and I knew that if anyone stepped out from the cover of those trees that they would stand a good chance of getting shot, themselves.

The Sheriff was left with but only one decision. He didn't want to but he had to burn them out. He told the boys to get to where they could get a clear shot of them when they came running out of the cabin.

He had made up some old rags and soaked them with lamp oil so they would burn for a while. Then he drawled back his bow and he had one of the men light it for him. When it had caught and was burning good, he shot the first arrow through the window that was on the front porch of the cabin.

He did the same thing over and over until he was out of arrows. As the men in the cabin tried to throw the burning arrows back outside. The boys picked them off as if they were flies on horse shit.

The cabin was made up of wood, so it didn't take much for it to start burning. It was just about fully in guff in flames when I couldn't help myself but to look over at Jamie and she was crying. This was hitting her hard but she never tried not once, to stop any of this from happening.

It was burning pretty good as some of the men came running outside of the burning cabin. They were firing their guns wildly as they tried to make a break for it.

They didn't get far when the boys shot them down.

They couldn't be too many of them left inside with Donald.

The men that were left inside threw their guns out and then they came running outside. They rather face us than burn to death, I guess.

The Sheriff told the men not to shoot and the men gave themselves up without a fight. We now had about ten of Donald's men in custody. They said that there was about ten more of them left inside of the cabin with Donald.

"I ask them" "if Donald was still in there?"

They said, yes but he has done lost his mind.

They said that he would die in there before he would ever give up.

The Sheriff said, not today. He will not die in that fire. He was not getting off that easy I assure you all of that.

I turned and look at the Sheriff when he said that. I knew that look that he had in his eyes all too well.

The Sheriff took off before I could stop him and he ran like the wind and jumped straight through the burning front door, right into the fire. He was going to drag Donald out by his feet if he had to.

All that we could hear was gunfire coming from inside of that cabin and the sound of the cabin falling down as it continued to burn.

Someone inside of the cabin was yelling that we give up. It was so quiet for the next few moments and then the Sheriff and Donald and four of his hired hands came out of the cabin just as the roof fell in.

When the Sheriff brought Donald and those men out to where we were standing at. I smacked him across his face and then before he could react to what I had just done to him. I hugged him and I kissed his face.

"Don't you ever try something like that again I told him?"

He said that, he wouldn't and that he loved me to, he thinks he said to me, as he rubbed his jaw.

The rest of us could now rest for a spell as we watched the cabin burning all the rest of the way to the ground. The smoke and the sound from all the firearms and shells that they had inside was going off as the fire got hotter and hotter.

We waited for the fire to die down some more and then we got back to business. There was no way that we were going to take those men back through that pass with all that snow covered peaks. Donald would have done something to cause an avalanche that would kill us all and we knew it.

Donald was planning on us taking him back because he told the Sheriff that it was a long way back to the Jailhouse.

The Sheriff corrected him and he told him really fast that he nor his men would ever see our little town again.

Donald looked shocked when the Sheriff had said that to him.

Donald knew what the Sheriff meant when he told him that. He told the Sheriff and myself that we couldn't do that. He said that he had to stand trial for what he had done in a court of law.

The Sheriff told him that he didn't give the people that chance of life when he killed all of them at his ranch.

The Sheriff said I tell you what I will do if you can find one person here that thinks that you should not hang for those two big oak trees. I will take you back to stand trial in a court of law. "Donald ask," "can I take you at your word Sheriff?"

The Sheriff said to Donald, I give you my word that no one here will harm you if someone stands up for you, that is.

Donald just knew that his daughter Jamie and her man Peyton would stand up for him.

The Sheriff stood faces to face to all of our gang and he repeated what he had told to Donald. "If anyone of you are willing to save this man's life, let him speak now or forever be silent." That's all the Sheriff had to say.

The Sheriff and I looked around at the crowd and they were looking at each other but only one person spook up.

"It was Jamie, Donald daughter." "I have something to say about all of this Sheriff, she said!"

Some of the men started yelling and guessing as she walked over to where the Sheriff and I were standing at with her father and his men.

The Sheriff told them to keep quiet and let the lady speak her mind.

Jamie walked up to the Sheriff and her father and then she spoke.

"She said, Father, I can't help but still tell you that I love you. You are after all, regardless of what you have done, you will be the only father that I will ever have. Make no mistake father, I am but a lady and not a God. I will show you as much compassion as you showed all those people that you destroyed there at our family's Ranch. You of all people deserve the judgment that all these fine people are going to dish out to you and your men. Hell is where you all belong!"

She turned her back to Donald and then she told the Sheriff and me that she had said, what she needed to say.

"She was in tears as she walked away but then Peyton walked over to where she was and he put his arms around her and he told her that he loves her and he had forgiven her for all that she had done to him."

The Sheriff look back at Donald and he was as quiet as a mouse as the Sheriff told the crowd to make them all swing.

The crowd took them all and they were so many of them that they had to use two different trees and they threw ropes across all of the bottom limbs which was still way off the ground. They lined their horses up side by side and sat them in their saddles for the last time. Then they spooked their horses from out underneath of them all except for Donald.

"They made him watch as his hired hands all lost their lives for the evil that they had done. Then it was Donald's turn."

The Sheriff had put the painted horse and the saddle with the silver saddle horn's on it underneath of him and the Sheriff was taking his sweet old time, just to add to Donald's fear of what was about to happen to him. He wanted for Donald to see all that he had caused, but Donald was not that kind of man.

"He kicked his own horse and it took off running from out underneath of him. He had gotten his way after all. He didn't wait for the crowd to hang him. He hung himself." They hung Donald and all of his men there in that valley, that very day.

We all made it back home and we had a safe trip all on account of Jamie. When we made it to town, they all walked up to Jamie and they told her that they too forgave her and they wanted her and Peyton to stay in our town forever more.

Well, people now you know our town's worsted nightmare and now you can understand why we have a black spot that we here in our town, will never forget for as long as we all shall live.

I have some more tells that I will tell you, at a later date. Watch out for them.

"Love Hazel and the Sheriff."

"Until next time!"

My name is Dallas Dwayne Conn. I am almost fifty years old. I have been writing for as long as I can remember. I have written a lot of stories and as soon as I got them done, I would throw them out with the trash. They were mine and I really didn't care to show them to anyone. I felt that they were private and belong to no one but me. I could always find a way to become anyone and anything. For me, it was a way to hide out from the real world. There you could become a superstar or a slave, even a man or women. I never knew who or what I was going to be until I sat down and started to write. I love the fact that as long as I was writing the story, no one else's opinion really mattered. I was in control of my own world. No one could tell you what to do in that world but yourself. I had been doing this for my whole life. It was how I made sense of the world that we live in. When I am writing, I can become anybody or anything. I wrote all types of books, from love stories to slasher books. The more blood, the better is what my son would say. I was just a big nobody and until I accepted that, I just had a lot of stories bouncing around in my mind. Then one day I put an idea on paper. That was that, I was hooked! I knew that my writing was how I could go anywhere and be anybody. It set me free, you could say. My mother told me not to listen to what people said about me but to give them something to talk about. That way they could say what they wanted to say but if they told the truth, you are the one in control and happy. People always will talk. The key was to control what they were talking about. If it was the truth, then it was good news, but people don't like to talk about good news as much as they like to speak about the bad news. All that you had to do is listen only to what you wanted to. You can zone the whole world out, at least, the part you didn't like and rewrite it the way it should have been to start with. That was what makes "you, you and them, them." I never knew what she meant, when she said that to me until I met and married my better half. Her name was Cassandra M Lewis, now she is a Conn. That name never did me any good so I gave it to her for her last name. That was thirty years ago. She taught me how to be me. That sounds funny but without her pushing me to write and quit throwing the stories away, you would never meet me. I will always be in her debt for that. I want to dedicate this book to her and my mother, Thelma Conn. "My mother was my first teacher and my wife is still teaching me." They are the two that made me the man that I am today. If you don't like it, you can take it up with them. I am disabled now and always in pain, except when I am writing. I can escape by taking myself anywhere in the world that I want to go. I don't even have to leave the house to do so. Remember it only takes you and your imagination. So don't let no one stop you from traveling the world.

THANK YOU

DALLAS DWAYNE CONN

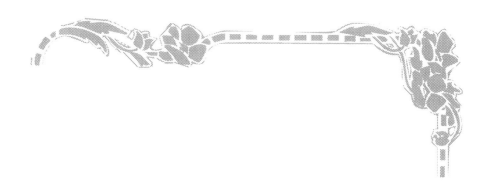

BOOK NUMBER FOUR

WHO DID IT AND WHY?

This is another story coming to you all from Hazel and her man the Sheriff. They have found themselves in another mess. The greed of some people takes Hazel away from her man and friends. The Sheriff goes after them and he is really pissed off at the way and why they would touch his women. The Sheriff will take you on the hunt for his women and he will have to solve the question of why someone would do what they did before he can find Hazel. You will love the twists that this story takes and what he puts the guilty ones through because of the reasons that they did what they did. He takes great pleasure in his work this time. Don't make the Sheriff mad because he won't stand for it. This time, he takes charge and even Hazel can't stop him.

By Dallas Dwayne Conn

You will love this one.

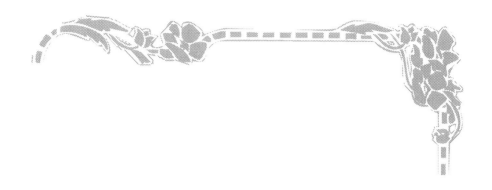

CHAPTER ONE

WHO DID IT AND WHY?

One day out of nowhere, there was this man that show up at Hazel's Diner, "by the way my name is Hazel", and he was wearing a suit of all things. You talk about standing out in the crowd. He looked so, out of place. Around here we didn't have no obvious use for a suite that much is for sure. The only time that someone had a suite on around here was when we were burying them. People here wore work clothes or something that they could wear while shoveling horse crap and then they would wash their hands and ride their horses to Church on Sunday. People just didn't care what you had on just so it hid all of your junk that you had in your trunk hidden.

This well-dressed fool, just walk into my diner and he just walked around and was looking at the place. He didn't say nothing to nobody he just keeps on gawking at my diner. He just keeps on walking around as if he had lost his best friend. Everybody that was in the diner stopped what they were doing and started to watch him as he walked around my place as if he owns it. I have had all of this, that I was willing to put up with for now. He was starting to get on my nerves.

"I walked over to where he was and I asked him," "what the hell was he looking for?"

"Did you lose something like your mind" "I ask him?"

He just looked at me and then he introduce himself to me and he said my name is Willis Smith.

Like that name was supposed to mean something to me. I told him that, he was going to have to do better than that because that name doesn't mean nothing to me. People around these parts know me as Hazel. This Diner that has seemed to catch your full attention belongs to me.

"I got to ask you, Mr. Willis Smith," "what in the world are you looking for?"

I represent the landholders of America Willis said to me, right cocky like. I was sent here by them, to see if you would be interested in selling your business. Willis told me that he has been authorized to pay top dollar for you little diner if you want to sell it to me.

"Hazel, ask Willis," "what would someone like you, not to say anything bad about your company, want with this old Diner?"

Willis said that the people that he works for wants this land that your Diner is setting on, to build a hunting log on. Just stop and think about how much that Hunting Lodge will help you all out around here. It would bring in a lot of new jobs for your neighbors and family.

"Where did the likes of you come from," "I ask Willis?"

Willis said that he was sent here from New York.

I am so sorry that you have had to travel so far, for nothing but my place is not for sale.

Willis told me that, his bosses have given him permission to pay top dollar for my place if I wanted to sell it.

Maybe you didn't hear me the first time Willis, I said to him. This place is not for sale at no price. "Besides what would I do with that kind of money around here," "I told Willis?"

He had the balls to tell me that with as much money that he was willing to pay me for my diner. I could travel around the world. Willis said that I could afford to set back and relax for a long while. Just think about it Willis said to me.

I told him that, I have seen enough of this world, to make me want to stay right here. I going to tell you just one more time and that's it, so listen up Willis. This place is not for sale at no price.

Willis told me that he was the type of man that doesn't take no for an answer. When they send me after something, they know that I will not stop until I get what I came for. Well, I am here to tell you, Willis, this time, you're going to leave empty hand. You won't be buying my Diner no time soon Willis that much you can bank on.

Willis told me that he would get my Diner that much, I could count on.

Now you just had to go there, didn't you, I told Willis. Now you have done and went and done it now, Willis. You have made me mad. I don't like to be made crazy this early in the morning. You just don't know who you are fooling with. Let me tell you something about the kind of person that you are talking to. I shoot and asked questions from your next of kin. Now that you know who you are actually dealing with. I will give you a matter of seconds, for you to get yourself out of my diner or I am going to start shooting and if you had bother to ask anyone, who you are trying to do business with, you would know that I will do what I say. You can tell that to the Land Holders of the American. Make sure you tell them that I said that. Know I said get and I do mean it.

Willis said that, we must have gotten off on the wrong foot and that he would like to start all over again.

There's no need for that Willis, I told him, so save your breath because you'll going to need it to run. I pulled out my pistols and I walk right up into his face and I keep on walking as he had no choice but to walk backward right out of my front door. When I had walked him outside to the street. I told him, there is your horse that you rode in here on and I am telling you now, that you'd best get your butt back on to your saddle and head out of here while you still can.

Willis look at me and he said but Mam.

But Mam my rear end, I told Willis. Only my friends, say that to my face. Since we don't know one another. The hell with you two. Now I told you to leave and I do mean for you to do it now. "Don't you even want to hear how much I am will to pay for your Diner Hazel," "ask Willis?"

I told him that, the answer was still no. The problem with you city slickers Willis is, you all don't listen to well. Your tie must be too tight or something is wrong with you that you are not getting it. Maybe this will clear it up for you. I opened fire up, right at his feet and that fancy dressed man, in his high dollar suit, jumped into his saddle and he was out of here. He knows now that I mean business, I'll bet you.

The Sheriff was over at the Jailhouse where his office was when he had heard all the gunfire that was coming from the Diner and he came a running to see what was going on.

"He asks me," "what was happening?"

I told him that I was just cleaning house. I had a few variant to get rid of this morning and I did it.

"With your guns," "Hazel," "asked the Sheriff?"

Yes, this one variant just didn't want to take no for an answer. Don't worry Sheriff, I said. This well dress variant took a little while but he finally got the picture. We will not see the likes of him around here no time soon. That is if he knows what's good for him. Some people just don't know when to take no for an answer.

"Who was he Hazel," "the Sheriff asked?"

He is just a big nobody I said, to the Sheriff. Just a land developer that's all. Just go back to what you was doing and leave the rest up to me dear. I gave the Sheriff a kiss on the lips and sent him on his way.

One day Hazel those guns of yours will get the best of you yet, the Sheriff told me.

I never saw that man again and it has been a couple of months of peace and quiet around here and we were all enjoying it so much.

It was late in the afternoon and the Diner there at Hazel's place was full of people. They were enjoying each other's company or at the least Hazel's open bar. Hazel and the Sheriff was enjoying their friends, as they were all celebrating their one year wedding anniversary.

To Hazel and the Sheriff, James toasted. You have made it a whole year or might we all say the Sheriff has. That was the toast the "James the town's mayor" had made to the lucky couple. "Hazel turned and she asked James," 'what did you mean when you made that toast, like that James?

James looked as if, I was going to "shoot him", for what he had said. That's when James told us about the bet that the whole town had going on.

I told James that, he'd best start spilling his guts right about now and he best not leave anything out and I mean it. I was pissed off and James knew that I was.

James said that the whole town was betting that I would shoot the Sheriff before the first year was out. Hazel we all was betting that you would get pissed at the Sheriff and kill him off. You know Hazel that you do have one heck of a temper, James said. It seemed like a sure winner Hazel, James told her.

The looks that I gave the mayor was not at all beautiful. You could hear a pin drop in my Diner because it had gotten so quiet. Everyone was just waiting to see what I was going to do when James told me that. They were all waiting to see what I was going to do. That struck me as funny and I just looked around and I thought that I would have some fun with them for a change. I walked to the middle of the floor so everyone could see me clearly. I put both of my hands on my hips and then I drawled my pistols out of my holster and I unloaded both of my guns into the ceiling. People just started to run out of the front door as if their pants was on fire and the back doors too. I acted as if I was out of my mind. I just broke down and started to laugh as the

Sheriff asked me" "what the Hell," "did I think I was doing by shooting wildly like that?"

They were making fun of us dear, I told the Sheriff, so I thought that it was about time, that I had some fun at their expenses. I was standing there busting a gut because I was laughing so hard. The Sheriff saw me as I was in tears because I had thought that this whole thing was so funny. Then he couldn't hold his laughter back either, because he to now, thought that what I had done was funny too.

The Sheriff told me that, he had never seen someone clear a room so fast in his lifetime.

I put my pistols back into their holster and I hugged my husband, the Sheriff and I told him that this was the best anniversary party that I had ever seen. The Sheriff and I were embraced in each other arms.

"That is when the Sheriff "ask me" "if I would like to dance with him?"

I told him that it would be my honor to dance with the man that I loved more than life its self. We were dancing all around the room when James and a few others came back to the Diner where we were dancing. They had a very strange look on their faces as James walked up to where the Sheriff and I were dancing. I told James, not to be so serious because I was only joking when I fired off my guns earlier. James said that something bad had happened. Hazel, it's really bad James said.

I stopped dancing with the Sheriff and I looked at James and all the other people and I said that someone best be talking. I said that I want to know just exactly what is going on and I do mean now.

James said that "Fred had been shot!"

"When I asked?"

He was shot when you were firing off your guns Hazel.

"Are you telling me that I killed Fred," "James?"

It looks that way Hazel.

I couldn't have shot him because I fired my pistols into the ceiling I told them all.

James said that Fred was on the upper balcony.

"What was he doing up there," "I asked James?"

The Sheriff and I went outside to see what they were all talking about. Sure enough, there was Fed's body and he had been shot.

I best stop here and tell you all who I am. My name is Hazel and I am married to the Sheriff. We are the ones that solve all the crimes that happen in our part of the world. I work side by side with my husband the Sheriff and we fight crime together that happens around these parts that we all call our home. We live in a little outpost town called Maple Wood. Our town is just on the outskirts of Yellow Stone National Park. It is wild around here at times but we all love it here. There is still some Indian tribes around these parts and my husband is part Indian. The chief of the Indian tribe is called Silver Cloud. He is the Sheriff, blood brother. The time period of this tell that I am telling you happens around the thirties and the forties. We still use our guns and our horses more than cars and trucks. Around here people trust and use their horses a lot more than cars or trucks. You have to be rich to afford a car or a truck to start with. People around these parts just don't have a lot of money to start with. We like to "shoot first" and ask questions, after the fact. So I will be telling you all this story to you. Set back and enjoy the ride as I explain why they think that I was the one that shot Fred.

The Sheriff called for the Medical Examiner. He wanted him to take a look at Fred's body. The sheriff told the M.E. to pull an all-nighter if he had to so he could find out fast who actually had shot Fred. He was just doing what he had always done so many times before and he had to go by the law. He said, to me that he had to take my guns from me just until this mess is cleared up. He told me that he knew that I had not shot Fred but he still had to enforce the law.

I knew that and I took off my holsters and both of my pistols and I gave them to him. I couldn't help but to feel as if I was necked standing there, without my guns strapped around my waist. I had always worn my guns and now I was without my best friends. Around here your guns was your best friends and you needed them just to stay alive.

"Could this actually be happening to me," "I thought to myself?"

The Sheriff told me that he would give my guns back to me after the M.E. gets the report back to me. As for now, Hazel, you were the only one that had fired a shot that we know of and I have no choice but to place you under arrest, for the murder of Fred Miller. The Sheriff had tears in his eyes as he walked me over to the Jailhouse and put me into a jail cell. I am so sorry Hazel my dear, the Sheriff said, but you know that I have to do this. If we don't follow the law, Hazel, then no one else would take us serious the Sheriff said.

I knew that he was right and so did the Sheriff. I told him that he was doing the right thing and he didn't have to say that he was sorry for doing his job. I told him that he was doing the right thing and he knows it and I know that he didn't have any other choice but to do his job. After everything had settled down and the Sheriff and I had gotten a chance to talk this whole thing out. I had to come up with the only reason that I could think of for this mess that I was in. I know where and how I fired my guns off. There is no way that one of my bullets could have hit Fred. He was on the upper front porch and I shot my guns off into the middle of the Dining room ceiling. He was nowhere near where I had shot. Maybe one of my bullets hit a nail and ricocheted off and hit him that way. That's the only way that I could have killed him. Regardless, I am in one hell of a mess. The only reason that I could come up with was that I was somehow being set up. By who and why was the question that we have to answer somehow. Right now I just don't know how to answer those questions that really need to be answered. "The Sheriff said," "by how and why, not to mention who would go to this much trouble Hazel," "just to set you up for murder like this?"

"What would someone have to gain by doing this to you Hazel of all people?"

Then I remembered something. That variant, which I ran off a while back. He was really mad when I refused to sell my Diner to him. He told me that he always got what he came for and he really did want my Diner. It has to be him I thought. His name was Willis Smith. "Hazel asked the Sheriff," "do you remember about two mounts ago when I told you about him?"

The Sheriff said "I think so."

That's when that real-estate man, tried to buy my place and how mad that he had gotten when I refused to sell out to him Sheriff I told him.

Yes, the Sheriff said, now that you mention it, I seemed to remember that.

"The Sheriff," "ask Hazel," "didn't he tell you, that he wanted to tear down you place and build a hunting lodge?"

Hazel told the Sheriff, yes he did.

But he was mad Hazel, but he left and he has not been seen around here, since then, as far as I know.

"The Sheriff ask," "he hasn't tried to get back in touch with you since then, has he Hazel?" "No" but that type of a man doesn't quit until he gets what he wants. Something tells me that he is behind all of this. He sure was determined to get my Diner that day, that's for sure. All that we have to do is prove it somehow. Don't tell no one go and get in touch with the one man in this town that would know if he is still around these parts. If he is trying to buy other people out James will know about it. I am talking about James and how much he likes to spread gossip. If something is happening around these parts, he would know about it before the rest of us would have anyhow. Everyone around here thinks, I am noisy but I don't hold a feather to that man's rear end. If there isn't nothing for him to talk about, he will make something up. There is something that tells me that we are on the right trail Sheriff. The reason that I know that it is him that is setting me up is he would be the only one that has anything to gain from me going to jail. He knows that, if I am in jail, that I would have to sell him my Diner just to pay for my defense.

The Sheriff told Hazel that he would get everything that we would need for us both to stay there in the Jailhouse together tonight. It's not how I was planning on spending our anniversary, Hazel, but we still will be together, the Sheriff said.

Hazel said, "you will do no such thing Sheriff," and he looked so confused when she told him that. You need to stay over there in the

Diner. If there is going to be something, happen to it. It will be tonight. What better way to get me to sell out than to burn my place down. That way he would be able to buy me out and for a heck of a lot less. He knows that I would not hesitate to take his offer because I would not have the money to rebuild the Diner back. He has the most to gain from all this and I just know that Willis Smith is our man. You didn't see him Sheriff, but I did. He told me that he didn't stop until he got what he wants. I could see it in his face. He just knew that I would jump at the chance to sell my Diner to him. A man like that would do whatever it takes to get whatever he wanted. That makes him out to be the worst kind of man in my books. That kind that takes whatever he wants one way or another.

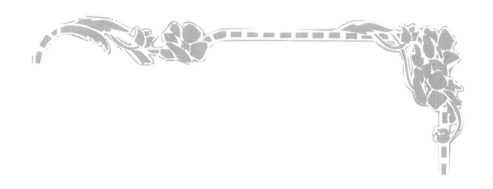

CHAPTER TWO

THE HIDEOUT

I didn't want to but I knew that Hazel was right this time. Hazel and I had talked it over and now we had come up with a plan. It was time to put it into place. If someone were setting Hazel up, they would think that she was out of the way now that she was in jail and it sure would be a great time for the diner to go up into smoke. I knew that if that happened. Hazel would lose everything that she owns in this world with one strike of a match. If it was that real-estate man, like Hazel was already thinking, "Willis Smith." Then he would win and get what he wanted to start with. Hazel just knew that he was behind this whole thing but we both knew that he was not doing this by himself. I knew and so did Hazel that he had to have somebody here in Maple Wood helping him do this. Nobody just shows up one day and wants to by a diner, just so they could take it down and build a hunting lodge. I knew that that just didn't happen. Somebody was helping him do this in our town and I was going to find out who was behind this.

Hazel wanted me to set a trap for the one that was reasonable for putting her into Jail. I knew that she didn't kill Fred and so did Hazel. She would never have fire her guns off like she did if she had thought that someone might have really gotten hurt. Hazel was only playing around and I know that she didn't mean anything bad by what she was doing when she did it. She was smarter than that. If Hazel and I were going to find out who's was really behind this, we were going to have to catch at least one of them in the act so that we could question them. Hazel was excellent at getting someone to talk but first we had to find someone to talk to and I knew that.

I didn't want to leave her in jail but I done as she had ask of me. Hazel had asked for me to go back over to the diner to watch over it and she wanted me to stay there while she had no choice but to remain in the Jailhouse. I had done given her an extra key to her jail cell and I told her to hide it so if she had to let herself out for some reason, she would be able to. I had put a gun into my bottom desk door. She was set and now it was my turn to get set up.

I was going to turn on all the lights in the diner on, to let everyone know that nothing had changed just because Hazel was locked up in

Jail. I had found a hiding spot in the back of the dining room, to where I was going to be hiding at. I could see everything and no one could see me. I had found a perfect spot to hide out and watch, without being seen myself.

The front of the dinner was full of windows. I could see straight out to the street that was in front of the diner. There was no way that anyone could see me from my hiding spot and they couldn't even get close to the diner without me seeing them first. The front porch was made of wood and it wrapped all the way around the front of the diner and down both sides of it. If anyone stepped onto the porch, I would be able to hear their footsteps.

The back of the diner, Hazel could see it from where she was at, in her Jail cell. Hazel's cell had a window that opens up and from where it was, she could see the back of the diner. So all four sides of the diner were now covered.

The first night nothing happen and that really surprised me. I thought that for sure if anyone were going to do something to the diner, they would have done it the first night, but they didn't. What were they waiting on I wondered? The next morning the cook show up and he wanted to know if Hazel and I still wanted him to open the diner up for business.

I told him that nothing had changed and he should do the same thing that he had always done. Business, as usual, I told Edd. Just because Hazel is in the Jailhouse, that doesn't change how we are going to do our jobs. So I help him opened the doors up for business, just like we had done so many times before.

Edd was Hazel's cook. He has worked for Hazel for years. He was more than capable of running the diner all by himself. Edd was a strong, tall man and he knew how to handle himself with his fist or a gun. It didn't matter to him. He knew that Hazel and the sheriff both trusted him there in the store by himself.

I helped Edd get started and then I went over to the M.E. office at the hospital. I wanted to see what kind of bullet that had killed Fred. The M.E had been working all night long on Fred's body as a favor to me. I had given him Hazel's guns and he used them to test if the bullet that killed Fred came from her guns.

The M.E. name was Bill Yates. Bill had said, that the test that he had done proved that Hazel's guns was not the one that had killed Fred. Bill told me that Fred had been killed with a twenty-two rifle. The bullet had entered his chest and hit his heart. The shot that killed Fred caused him to bleed out in a matter of seconds and that was what killed him. He was dead before he hit the ground. The M.E said, that the test that he had run proved that Hazel was innocent of this crime. He told me to go and get Hazel out of the Jailhouse and he also said that you two now have another murder to solve.

I just couldn't help myself and I gave Bill a great big hug.

Bill told me to stop that and go get your wife.

I went straight back to the jail to tell Hazel the good news. Hazel was still locked up and I was now going to set her free because Bill had said that we had another murder to solve now. When I had made it to the Jailhouse. I barged into the Jailhouse and I went right to the cell block where Hazel was at. I walk into the cell block and I was shouting out loud, the good news that Bill had told me, so Hazel could hear me but when I had gotten there to her cell, Hazel was nowhere to be found.

"What in the devil is going on here," "I ask myself?"

"Where was Hazel at, I couldn't help but to wonder?"

I thought that someone had already been there and they must have let her lose or she had used that spare key that I had given her to hide. Now that I knew she was not in the Jailhouse. I ran over to the diner. That was the only other place that she could have gone. When I had gotten there, she was not there neither.

"What is going on?"

"Where is my wife at," "I ask Edd?"

He told me that he had not seen her since last night.

"Did you check upstairs to see if Hazel had gone up there Sheriff," "Edd ask?"

"I ask everybody" "if they had seen Hazel when I couldn't find her upstairs?"

"I ask anyone that I saw if they had seen her but no one had laid eyes on her this morning Sheriff" "they all said?

I knew that she couldn't have just vanished into thin air but no one knew where she was. I stopped looking for Hazel for a moment and caught my breath. I had to calm myself down when I couldn't find her. I was just working myself into a panic by acting the way that I was. Fear was taking me over and I had to stop it, from doing so. I was not doing her no good acting the way that I was nor was I helping myself out by acting that away. I was just driving myself insane. I stopped and cleared my head out so that I could gather my thoughts together and clear my head out enough to think where she could possibly be at.

I knew that she could take care of herself, no matter where she, may be at. I had given her an extra key to her Jail cell and she knew that there was another gun in my desks, bottom door. I went back over to the Jailhouse after talking to Edd and he had told me, that he had not seen her this morning. I knew that she was all right and I thought that she had set herself free.

"She had left the Jailhouse but where did she go from there I ask myself?"

I had to make sure. I walked over to my desk and checked the bottom door for that gun that I put in there last night. Low and behold there was that gun that I had put there the night before and it had not been touched.

"What is going on here, I thought to myself?"

"Where in the world could she had gone?"

Now I was starting to worry about her wellbeing. I went to the cell block there in the Jailhouse and I was looking for that extra key that I had given to her the night before to hide. I found that spare key right off. She had not even used it. I had given it to her to hide just in case she need to set herself free for some reason but it was still there where I saw her hide it. I looked on the wall to where I keep all the other keys at and they were now gone. I knew then that she was in trouble because something had happened here and I knew it deep down inside of myself. She would have never left that Jailhouse without letting me know first. Now I was very worried about her. I walked out back of that Jailhouse where I keep the horses at and there was her horse. In the stables that were out back of the Jailhouse. If she had left on her own, she would have taken her own horse. Hazel would never have gone anywhere without that old gray nag of hers.

"What was going on around here, I thought to myself?"

My mind was going wild with fear as I had gotten more and more worried about Hazel. There was something very wrong with this whole thing. She would have never left the Jailhouse without letting me know something. There would have been some sort of a note or something like that but I couldn't find nothing. I knew that she wouldn't have never left the Jailhouse without leaving me something behind so that

I wouldn't worry about her like this. She must have been taken out of her cell by someone.

"But who would have taken her from the Jailhouse like this, I ask myself?"

I went back to where she was in the Jailhouse at and I searched her Jail cell once more. When I pulled the blanket back that was on her cot, my "heart skipped a beat". There was blood on her bed. I knew then that she was most definitely taken against her will. I could tell that she had put up a fight and somehow she was hurt or that blood wouldn't be there in her bed like that. I just knew that blood had to have been Hazels. I was trapped by fear and I felt so helpless.

For the first time in my life, I found myself, feeling like there was nothing that I could do to help Hazel. I was now helpless to her and I knew it. If I was to leave town to search for my wife. Whoever took her from the Jailhouse would eventually destroy the dinner, I thought to myself. That is if it was whom Hazel and I thought it was to start with. I had never laid eyes upon Willis' face, so I didn't know who he was and I couldn't find him even if I wanted to, just because I didn't know what he really look like.

Money will drive most men mad if they will let it. If there was money to be made here, then Hazel's life was surely in grave danger. I went back outside of the Jailhouse to where the stables were at and fresh tracks were coming and going from the back of the Jailhouse. They couldn't have been, but a few hours old.

Hazel and I had been watching the diner when we should have been looking after the Jailhouse but that something that we just didn't know. Hazel and I were trying to set a trap for them and they set one for us instead. I knew then that whoever that was behind all of this. Had set both Hazel and me up. They had killed Fred and framed Hazel, just so they could split us up and they would have available assets to Hazel. She was who they were after the whole time and we just didn't know that. They had planned to split Hazel and me up all along. If it was, that man called Willis. There is one thing that he had not planned on. He had done went and made me angry. If I know Hazel and I do, she would give them hell. Hazel just don't know when to back off sometimes. I just hoped that she has not made them mad enough, to where they have done already had killed her.

Hazel woke up with her head hurting her, really bad. She reached her hand up to the top of her head and there was blood coming from a cut, which she had, on the back of her head. That is when she had remembered that Willis had hit her with his gun, to knock her out. She looked around and saw that she was in an old abandon barn. She didn't have a clue to where they had brought her to. She couldn't see outside because she was tied up to the middle support post, in the barn. I looked around for something that might help me somehow escape but there was nothing there close enough for me to get my hands on, that would help me get free. Whoever had put me here tied my leg to that center post with a chain. I was being held there just as if I was an old dog or something like that. Someone was coming so I laid back down and acted as if I had not woken up to start with. I was hoping that I might get the jump on them if they get close enough to me.

They opened the barn door and came inside to where I was tied up at. They took some water that was in a bucket and threw it into my face. They used it to wake me up so I played along with them. I acted as if they had startled me with that water, so I jump just like they would have expected me to do so. When I opened my eyes, there he was. It was just who I had thought it was this whole time. It was Willis and another man was with him. Wakey, Wakey Hazel my dear Willis said to Hazel.

"Why in the world would you do this to me," "Hazel ask Willis?"

Willis told Hazel that she should already know the answer to that question before you even ask me that. I have done told you, Hazel, that I always get what I want.

"Don't you remember what I told you, the first time that we met Hazel, Willis ask Hazel?"

"Yes, I do" but do you remember the answer that I gave to you and what it was," "Hazel ask Willis?"

"Yes," Willis said. It was the wrong answer then and it still is now Hazel, Willis told her.

"What makes you think," "that I am going to change my mind now," "Hazel ask Willis?"

Because if you don't change your mind now, I will kill your beloved Sheriff. If you think that I want then try me, Willis told Hazel.

"Like you killed Fred," "Hazel ask Willis?"

Yes Hazel, just like I killed Fred. You are not seeing the whole picture, Hazel. I killed him just so I could get you and the Sheriff separated from each other. You see Hazel, I had this whole thing planned out from the start with. To a tee. I didn't leave nothing out. This time, you will do just what I tell you to do or, this time, I will kill the Sheriff but not in the same way that I killed Fred, Willis said Hazel. I will shoot him in front of you. I reached into my suit pocket and pulled out this paper. It was the bill of sales that I had for your diner. I told Hazel, that if you want to save the Sheriff's life, you will sign the diner over to me.

"Now," "what makes you think that's going to happen?"

Because I am not asking you, this time, Hazel, I am telling you to, Willis told Hazel. If you don't, I'll kill the Sheriff and then I will kill you as well.

"Do you think that I am stupid" "Willis", "ask Hazel?"

If I sign that dead of sales to my diner over to you Willis, you will still kill me and if I don't you will still kill me anyhow, Hazel told him. So the way I look at it Willis, I am going to die either way.

"So why don't you go ahead and get it over with?"

"Come on and shoot me," "Willis?"

"What in the hell are you waiting for Willis?"

"I know you are afraid to do it yourself" "aren't you?"

"You don't have the balls to get blood on your own hands do you," "Willis?"

"What is it Willis," "is the problem as simple as you are afraid of getting blood on your fancy suit?"

"Let me asked you something, Willis?"

"What makes you think that you'll get away with this?"

He said, that's easy, I was never even here. I am still in the big city. I have about ten people that are willing to testify that I am home in the bed, with the flu. So you see Hazel, I am a man of my word. I always get what I want. I like being me.

I hate to let some of that hot air out of your big ego Willis, but you still don't know who you are dealing with. The Sheriff and I always get our man and we will get you for Fred's murder and for kidnapping me and holding me against my will. The Sheriff will come for me and when he does you will be sorry. You see people around here look after each other and someone will come for me, you just wait and see, Willis.

Willis got angry because when he reach that paper to Hazel so that she could sign it. Hazel tore it up instead of signing it. He drew his hand back and smacked Hazel, crossed her face.

I turned my head back around from where Willis had hit me and I told him that he would pay for that stupid move, that much you could bank on Hazel told Willis.

I knew that I had to go after Hazel and get her back home. Deep down inside of me, I know that she was in real danger. I know what to do. I will go and find James and see what he knows. Someone around here has to know something. If I know him, he is over at the diner because it is all most lunch time. If he is in on this, I will know it just as soon as I lay my eyes on him. I have to calm myself down. This is not the time for me to lose my head. Hazel is counting on me. I have to use my wits and cunning to trap the ones that are helping whoever is behind this whole mess. I walked over to the diner and I was acting as if nothing was wrong. I couldn't let anyone know that Hazel was gone because I don't know who I can trust. I saw James sitting at our usual table when I walked in.

"Sheriff" "James ask," "how's Hazel doing this morning?"

She is asleep I told James, but she is doing as good as to be expected. I look him right into his eyes.

"James ask me" "if anything was wrong?"

I knew then that he had nothing to do with her disappearance.

"I ask him" "if he had seen anyone else in the diner this morning?"

Know Sheriff James said I have been here for some time this morning and it's just been Edd and me. I guess that everyone thinks that the diner is closed because Hazel not here to open it up.

Edd was shaking his head and he told me that James has been the only one in this morning. "What was I missing I ask myself?"

Let me back up and think. I was at a loss for words. I had decided to go back over to the jail house and take a closer look at those tracks that I had seen early. When I got there, I notice something that I must have overlooked earlier. They were three different sets of horse tracks and then they was a set of boot tracks that was out of place.

"Now where did you come from and how did I miss you before," "I ask myself?"

Sheriff old man you are slipping, I said to myself. You should have seen this earlier I said to myself. I started to follow those tracks and they lead me to the back of the feed store. They went right into the back door. Whoever it was that was involved with that land developer, was here in the Feed store.

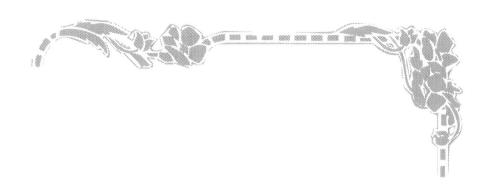

CHAPTER THREE

SO THAT'S WHO

I went back to the diner and I got James and Edd. I told them that I needed their help for a moment or two.

"Sheriff" "what about the diner" "Edd ask?"

"Do you want me to lock the door or what Sheriff" "ask Edd?"

No Edd I told him, just leave it the way that it is for now. I told them that, this won't take long at all boys.

James was just following after the Sheriff and Edd just like he was a lost puppy and James had a bowl of dog food for it.

James and Edd both knew that something was going to go down. They could only hope that it was not bad.

"Where are we going Sheriff," "Edd ask?"

I told them that, we are going to the feed store. Just shut up and follow me, I said. I need you both to witness something for me.

Edd and James just look at one another and keep on walking faster and faster, just trying to keep up with the Sheriff.

The Sheriff was in front and James and Edd was behind him as he opened the door to the feed store so fast and hard, that he looked as if he was going to tear it right off the hinges. They knew that look that the Sheriff had in his eyes. The Sheriff was out for blood. Somebody was about to get hurt and James and Edd knew it.

We all rushed in the Feed Store and Edd tried to stop the Sheriff or, at least, slow him down. Then James walked up behind the Sheriff and he took his guns out of the Sheriff's holster.

Give them back to me James I told him.

James said to the Sheriff, not until you tell us what is going on. Before I could answer him back.

I saw Sam Rogers making a dash for the back door when he saw me coming. I jumped right over top of Edd and I was all over Sam.

"Where do you think that you'll going Sam," "I ask him?"

I jumped across the counter top and I had my hands around his throat and I was trying to squeeze the life right out of him. That's when James and Edd pulled me off of him. I was screaming for them to let me lose. I wanted to kill him. Edd and James would not let me free regardless of how hard I begged them to.

"Why are you doing this Sheriff," "James ask me?"

Ask Sam, he knows why, don't you Sam I told them.

"What is the Sheriff talking about" Edd asked Sam?"

I don't know, Sam said.

You lying sack of horseshit, I said to Sam. I begged for James and Edd to let me go. I will tell you why I want this little piece of trash so bad if you two will get let me lose for a second. He knows who has Hazel. When I said that, Edd and James stilled didn't let me go. Instead, they held me even tighter. They knew that I wanted him to bad to trust myself with him.

One of those two said that someone better be talking right about now.

"Edd said Sam," "what is this man talking about?"

Edd told them that, I want to ask you again because if you don't start talking right now, I will let the Sheriff go. I would say that he will kill you right about now Edd said, to Sam.

Sam said don't let him go because he is a mad man. I'll talk. Just don't let go of him Edd, Sam begged of him. Please, Sam said again, to Edd.

I told Sam that if anything has happened to Hazel. I will kill you, but when I kill you. I will take my good old time and I will enjoy it. You know that my blood brother Silver Cloud has showed me a few tricks of the trade. I will kill you just like the Indians would have.

Sam told us that he would talk if we could keep the Sheriff from killing him. I will talk Sam said. I was approached by Willis Smith and he offered me a lot of money and he still wanted to buy my Feed Store from me too. He was going to pay me, even more, money for the Feed Store. You have to understand Sheriff, I am about to lose my store to the bank anyhow. I really needed the money and I need it fast. Somehow he knew that the bank was going to take my Feed Store from me. I would have lost everything if that happened to my family and me. I would have lost my house also. You see I had to put my house deed up for collateral when I bought this Feed Store. That's how he got me to help him to start with. Willis told me that we both could get rich and rich fast. That was the only way out for my family and Willis knew that. Willis told me that I didn't have a chose and I knew that he was right when he said that to me. Hazel was the only one that was standing in his way Willis told me, Sheriff. I have a family to think about also. With the money that, Willis was going to pay me. I was going to take it and move my family out east. With that money, my family and I were going to start a whole new life out there with my wife's family.

I didn't know that he was going to take Hazel. If I did, I would never have helped him in the first start. Willis didn't tell me about what he was planning on doing until it was too late. I was with him and one other man. I don't know who that man was. I just knew he was bad news. I have never seen him before that day. He never even spoke to me and Willis didn't tell me who he was. I didn't really care. We were out to the old Ricen place. Willis had given me some money there and all three of us rode back to town together. They wouldn't let me out of their sight. I feared for my life and for my family's life as well.

I thought that we was coming here to the store whenever we left the Ricen Farm but Willis wanted to go instead to the back of the Jailhouse. I thought that he just didn't want anyone to see us together and neither did I, Sheriff. When we all three had gotten there at the stables behind the Jailhouse. They told me to wait there and hold the horses. Sheriff, I did what I had to because I thought that they would have killed me if I didn't. You have to, believe me, Sheriff. I never intended for none of this to happen. Hazel and you Sheriff have both been good to my family and me. If I could have stopped all of this from happening to start with, trust me, I would have Sheriff.

"You know that I would never hurt Hazel," "don't you Sheriff?"

When he said that, I lunged at him once more but Edd and James still had too good of a hold on me. I just couldn't get to him and he knew that I wanted him extremely bad. I will get lose eventually and when I do, Sam. I am going to make you pay for what you have done to Hazel. The way that I look at it Sam, I told him, is you are even more at fault than Willis is and his hired hand is because you could have come to even Hazel or me. But you didn't. You just took the easy way out. It was easier for you to line your pockets with blood money than to do the right thing. That's what I will make you pay for, that you can count on. I give you my word on that.

Edd said, Sam, you better be telling the Sheriff all that you know and the rest of what he needs to know before I get tired and loosen my grip on him. We all know what will happen when he gets lose from me. I would tell the Sheriff everything if I was you, Sam, Edd said.

I am telling him everything that I know Edd, Sam said. When I was standing there with the horses. Willis and that other man went into the Jailhouse. I thought that they were just going to talk to Hazel. Just maybe I thought, that she might have changed her mind and signed the title to her Diner over to him because they were in there for a while.

Then I heard them fighting. They were yelling at each other one moment and then everything had gotten so quiet all of a sudden. I was really scared for Hazel when everything had gone so quiet. I knew then that someone inside that jail house had gotten hurt. I was just hoping against all odds that it wasn't Hazel, Sheriff. That is when they came back outside and they had Hazel with them. I thought that she was dead at first because she had blood on her head.

They brought her over to where I was at with the horses. When I help them put her on my horse, she moved. That is when I knew that they had just knocked her out just enough to where they could take her without a fight. It still took all three of us to put Hazel on my horse because she was now putting up a fight when they tied her hands to the saddle. Sheriff, I didn't want to help them do that to Hazel but Willis and the other man said if I didn't do as they had told me to, that they would kill me.

"Please Sheriff," "tell me that you believe me?"

I tried once more to get my hands on Sam, but Edd and James, wouldn't let me go.

James, told Sam, "to finish the story and fast."

"Okay" I will, Sam told them. After I help them put Hazel onto my horse. Then Willis told me to go home and I best not tell anyone if I know what was best for my family and me. I knew then that Willis would have his man come back and hurt my family if I didn't listen to what they had told me to do. After they rode off into the night. I went straight home and told my family to pack up everything and I sent them out of here this morning. They are on their way out east. That's where my wife's mother lives at. I told her that I would be there just as soon as Willis gave me the money for my store. I don't know if Willis took her to the same place where we first meet at or not. I wish that I knew more about their plans, but I don't Sheriff. That's all that I know Sheriff.

"The Sheriff ask, Sam," "did you leave anything out?"

"No sir," I told you everything that I know.

Let me lose, Edd and James, and you two take this trash and put him in Jail before I kill him myself. I would but I don't trust myself to be around him right now. Tell me something Sam.

"The Sheriff, ask Sam," "just how was Willis getting in touch with you?"

He would send word by that man that he had working for him when he wanted to meet with me. "The Sheriff, ask Sam," "was your place and Hazel's all that Willis said that he wanted?"

"No Sheriff," Sam said that if Willis could get Hazel's place. That Willis would be able to buy out everyone else's place here in town. Willis said that he wanted to buy every place out on Main Street. That way Willis would own every business on both sides of Main Street. Willis was then going to sell the land to the men that he was working for but at a larger profit. Willis planned on getting rich off of all that land. That was his plan and that's why I sold out to him. Willis said that he had always gotten what he wanted and anyone that would not sell to him. Willis said that he would send his men out to them and when he got done with them. They would sell out or Willis would take them out of the picture altogether. So you see Sheriff, I didn't have a choice but to sell out to Willis.

"That is where, you are wrong," the Sheriff told Sam. A man always has a choice in life to make. You just happen, to have made the wrong choice Sam, the Sheriff told him.

Edd and James took Sam over to the Jailhouse they locked him up as the Sheriff had told them to do.

You stay here Sam, and think about what you have done, Edd said.

"You too aren't going to stay here with me," "Sam ask?"

"Why" "Sam, ask James?"

What will happen if Willis or his hired hand comes back and finds me in here all alone, Sam ask?

That's one question, you should have thought about before you had gotten yourself involved with the likes of those two James said, as him and Edd walked out of the Jailhouse on their way back to the diner where the Sheriff was at.

The Sheriff had rung the towns Church bell. That bell only rang out on Sundays or in an emergency. Senses this was not Sunday, people came a running to see what was happening. The sound of that bell could be heard for miles around. It was just another way to call out for help when one of us needed help. We all watched out for one and another, so with everybody hearing the bell toll. They all stopped what they were doing and came a running as soon as they heard that bell ring out, into town. The Church was just down the street from the dinner and the Sheriff walked outside of the diner and he fired off a double barrel shotgun. It was deafening and when they all heard that blast from his gun, they all came to the diner where the Sheriff, James, and Edd was already at. The Sheriff put the shotgun down and he went to the edge of the front porch, there at the diner.

Everyone quite down, the Sheriff said.

The people stopped talking and they all listen to what the Sheriff had to say.

I am your all's Sheriff and Hazel has been taken from the Jailhouse against her will. There is a stranger in our midst and he was the one that had taken Hazel.

"When did this happen," "one of them from the crowd ask the Sheriff?"

This happened last night and I think that they are hold up, at the old Ricen place. I will need as many men as you all can spare, to form a Posse to go and get her back. Sam Rogers was involved in this mess and we can only go on what he has told me. He told me that Willis was out there with at least one other man but he couldn't be sure if more men were working with him.

The crowd said that they all would help. Just tell us what you need us to do and we will do it, Sheriff. You and Hazel have kept us all safe, for all these years. It's about time that we return the favor.

Be quite and I will tell you all what I know. There was this man called Willis Smith that wanted to buy Hazels diner and when she would not sell it to him. He told her that he would get it one way or another. I think that he was behind Fred's death. The M.E told me that Fred was not killed with Hazel's guns but instead he was shot with a Twenty Two Riffle. Fred was killed just to set Hazel up with his murder. Willis planned this whole thing out just to get her out of the way. He wanted her to be put into Jail so that he could take her from there. He knew that she would be left there by herself and he would not have to fight the whole town, just to get at her.

"What kelp Hazel from shooting him right then, when she had told him that she wouldn't sell out to him, "one of them ask the Sheriff?"

I think that she should have but she knows the law and so do you all. Enough with that kind of talk the Sheriff said, we need to go and get her now. This man will stop at nothing to get what he wants. That makes him very dangerous. I don't want none of you to run out there half-cocked and get yourself or anyone else hurt. So do as I say and not as you all want to do, okay. I wanted you all to know that I don't know how many people that he has with him, so we will be going in there blind-sided. So I want all of you to follow me and we will ride out there and see what we can find out. I want you all to stop just this side of where the Ricen place is and we will go on from there on foot. We need to get the jump on them and that way we will stand a better chance of taken them by surprise. I don't want no one to fire a shot until I find out where Hazel is at and if she is all right. If we can get to her and get her out of there before the shooting starts, we will. One way or another we will get Willis and I do know he has, at least, one man with him. So men do be careful and nobody gets hurt.

The Sheriff and all of the men rode their horses out to the Ricen place and they done just as the Sheriff had told them to do. They all stopped just before they all had gotten to the Ricen place. There the Sheriff had split them up into groups of ten. He sent them in all different directions. That way none of Willis men would stand a chance of getting away from them. All of the men wanted Willis and his gang, so they done just as the Sheriff had told them to do.

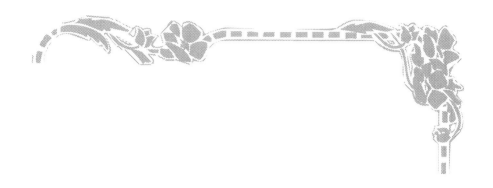

CHAPTER FOUR

THE RICEN FARM

The Sheriff had all the men where he need them to be. From where they were, at least, one of them could see every square inch of the Ricen farm. The old farm house was in terrible shape and they were no one that was staying in the main house. It was ready to fall down. No one had lived in it for a many of years. There was a bunkhouse that looked as if someone had been staying there, though. That was where everyone that worked for the Ricen family stayed at, a long time ago. The old barn had seen its better days but it was still standing somehow. If they had Hazel here, she had to be in one of those two buildings.

I had told all the boys that I had with me, to just lay low and I was going to see if anyone was home. I was trying to see if they had Hazel hid out here. I still didn't know if she was even here or Willis and his man, either. I slowly made my way over to the barn. I thought that if she were even there, that would be where they would be keeping her at. I snuck around to the back side of the barn but I couldn't really see the inside of the barn because they were some old hay left over from where the Ricen family had lived there. It was piled up to high for me to see over. I tried to make my way down the outer side of the barn, to see if I couldn't see inside the barn better. Just as I had gotten into place two men walked out of the bunk house and they were walking straight for the barn.

They walked over to the barn doors and then they opened it up. When they did that, they let light in the dark barn.

Then I was able to see Hazel. They had her tied up to the center post in the barn. I was so relieved to see that she was still alive. She was still Hazel as they tried to get her to sign over her diner. I knew then that she was all right.

Hazel told them that, I have done told you all that I won't sign that title and I mean it she said.

That's when I heard her call one of them Willis. I had never seen him so I didn't know what he looked like.

One of them told Hazel and the other man that was with them. That she knows what going to happen now. Hazel said, let me guess you are going to kill me now because you can't get me to sign that piece of paper for you.

Know Hazel Willis said, I am going to tell my man to go and shoot the Sheriff.

Hazel said that I know something that you don't. The sheriff will be here for me and he will be like a thief in the night. You'll not even see him until he wants you to. By that time, it will be too late. So go ahead and sent your man after him and we will see who makes it back here first. I just go ahead and I tell you that my money is on the sheriff.

Tell me something Hazel, Willis said. If you too are married to each other.

"Why do you still call him the Sheriff?"

"I'd tell you but then I would have to kill you if I did." Hazel just started to laugh at him and he was mad because of what she was doing.

Willis had heard that she was not afraid of nothing and he knew now that he had heard right.

I had heard enough and I knew that it was time for me to make my move. I eased my way around to the front of the barn and I was waiting for them to come out of the barn door.

The Sheriff had hid behind the barn door that they had open and they left it open when they went inside the barn. The Sheriff was there as they made their way outside. When the hired hand had walked away from the open door, then Willis reach his hand out to shut the door. When he did that, the Sheriff grabbed his hand and he twisted it behind of his back. The hired hand that was working for Willis didn't know what to think because it had happened so fast. When he turned around and saw the Sheriff and what he was doing. He had done had his gun in his hand and he fired at the Sheriff but instead of him hitting the Sheriff like he had planned on. He shoots Willis. Willis dropped down to his knees and the Sheriff opens fire on him before he could get another shot off. The Sheriff had killed the hired hand and the hired man had killed Willis. The Sheriff's men had heard all the gunfire and they come to the Sheriffs aid.

I told the men to check all the other buildings and I was going to get my wife.

The Sheriff went to the barn and there in the middle of the barn was Hazel. She was tied up to the center support post by her leg.

I walked over to where she was and she ripped me a new butt whole.

"I said," "why are you yelling at me like that Hazel?"

I want to know what in Gods good name, took you so long to come and get me, Sheriff.

I here now Hazel that is what really matters.

I guess you are right Sheriff.

"Where are Willis and his lap dog," "Sheriff?"

I told Hazel that they both were dead.

Hazel told me that was good.

"I asked, Hazel" "if she had seen anyone else?"

Hazel said that those two were all that she had seen since they tied her to that post in the barn. There has not been no one else here that I know of that is Hazel said. I am sure glad that it was only those two, Hazel said.

I am really glad Hazel. I reached down and held out the chain and I shot the lock off with my gun. Then I took that chain off of her leg. I reached down and help Hazel to her feet and she told me that she was so glad that this whole mess is now over with. Not just yet I said, to Hazel.

"What do you mean by that" "Hazel asked him?"

Sam Rogers had something to do with this, I told Hazel.

I know Hazel said to the Sheriff. He was there at the Jailhouse with Willis and his hired hand.

Yes, Hazel, I told her but he was not the only one that was in own this.

"Hazel asked the Sheriff," "what was I talking about?"

There is, at least, one more person that we have to talk about when we get back to town I told Hazel. "Hazel asked the Sheriff" "who it was?"

I don't know yet but I will find out when we get back to town, I told her.

The sheriff and all of his men searched the old Farm House and then they looked in the bunk house. There was nothing that tied Willis to no one back into town.

Hazel said that, if I were looking for any paperwork, it would be in Willis suite pockets. He put my land deed back inside of his suit pocket whenever I refused to sign it.

When Hazel told me that, I walked over to Willis dead body and there in his suit pocket was the deed for Hazels place and on the other side of his suite was some bank papers. This is what I am looking for the sheriff told Hazel. There are one more pieces of this puzzle that we need to address Hazel.

The men that went out there with the Sheriff said that they would finish cleaning up the mess out here if you want to take Hazel back to town Sheriff.

I would sure appreciate that if they didn't mind to doing that for Hazel and me.

Hazel and the Sheriff rode back to town and the Sheriff went straight over to the Jail to talk to Sam. When Hazel and the Sheriff got there, the Sheriff took Hazel inside of the Jailhouse to speak to Sam.

Sam told Hazel that he was so sorry for what he had done and he would never have done it if he knew that they were going to hurt her.

Hazel said that it was all right and she was all right now that they were back in town now. "Sam ask about Willis and his hired hand?"

That's when I told Sam, that they were both dead and that he didn't have to worry about those two again. That's not what we come over here to talk to you about I said. I said that you had told me something early.

"What Sheriff," "Sam ask?"

You told me that Willis knew that you were about to lose your feed store and your house.

Sam said yes Sheriff, I said that to you.

"What does that have to do with anything?"

I told Sam and Hazel that, it has a lot to do with this case. If someone over there at the bank, let anyone else know what kind of financial shape that you was really in there at the bank. Then they two was in on this with Willis. He couldn't have known anything about your banking business unless someone there at the bank had not already told him about you. That would mean that you Sam was set up from the start with.

I don't know who it could have been Sheriff, Sam told him.

I just need to hear that from you, just to make sure before Hazel and I go over to the bank. The good news is that you will not be sleeping along tonight, I told Sam. Then I told Hazel to come with me and we will finish this once and for all. I took Hazel by the hand and we went over to the bank and sure enough, there set Mark Hall.

He was the bank president. He was born and raised in New York. He had been moved here from the bank's central office. He never liked it here, though.

"He looked at the Sheriff and Hazel as if he had seen a ghost!"

"I saw him sitting there in his office. He was acting like he was some sort of a fattening hog, lying in a big puddle of mud. I just couldn't understand why some people never got enough money and power. People like that just make my blood boil. Friends and family are what the good Lord wanted us to collect not money and power. I couldn't help myself when I saw him. Something inside of me snapped. I tore through his front door which by the way, was made out of glass and it shattering it into a million pieces. I was all over him and there was no way that he could get me off. Regardless of how bad, he was trying he still couldn't stop me from hitting him. I was punching him, over and over again. I told him that I was just returning, just some of the hell, that he had put my family and friends though over the last couple of days. I told him that I knew that he was behind this whole mess. The reason that I knew that was he was the only one that stands to gain the most from this land deal. You were the one that put our town through hell just so you could line your pockets. I was like a wild tiger as I tore right into to him. I just wanted to rip his head off."

Don't try to deny it, because I have done seen your man Willis. He had a lot to say, I told him. He didn't know that I had not spoken directly to him, though. I didn't tell him that I spoke to Willis, I just said that Willis had a lot to say. The more that I beat him, the more that he said he did. He told everything on his self. Mark Hall had ratted out himself. He would have sold out his own mother just to get me off of him. Hazel and a few others that were there, help get me off of Mark Hall before I had taken it too far and actually killed him. I sure did want to for what he had done.

After they had all come together and gotten the Sheriff off of him. They had persuaded the Sheriff to spare his life, for at least, long enough for his and Sam's trail. They took him and put him in jail with Sam. The Sheriff was right when he had told Sam that he wouldn't be sleeping along at the Jailhouse no more. He now had a roommate. When the Sheriff and Hazel had gotten done with Mark Hall and they locked him up in a cell beside Sam. They went back over to the diner where their friends and family were waiting for their return.

They both walked into the Diner holding hands and they went over to their favorite table and sat down. All of their family and friends just set back and was now enjoying each other's company, yet once more. The whole town had pulled together and saved each other from the bad guys. That teamwork is what makes them all family. They had looked after each other and brought each other closer together.

They had done just like they had so many times before. They had all gotten their man. Life here in the Town of Maple Wood was back to the way it was supposed to be. Peaceful and quiet just the way they like it to be. Until the next crime happens.

Don't worry flocks, Hazel, and the Sheriff will always be ready to protect their way of life from those that want to take if from them. "Until next time love Hazel and the Sheriff!"

"P.S." Old Hazel has a lot more hair-raising tells up her dress tail that I will tell you when the Sheriff and I rest up for a spell. Keep your ears to the wind and listen for my call!

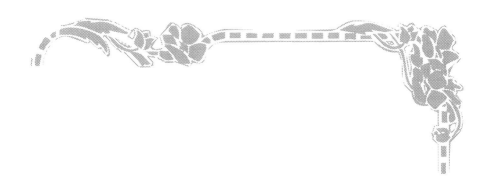

ABOUT THE AUTHOR

I have been writing for as long as I can remember. I have written a lot of stories, and as soon as I got them done, I would throw them out with the trash. They were mine, and I really didn't care to show them to anyone. I felt that they were private and belonged to no one but me. I could always find a way to become anyone and anything. For me, it was a way to hide out from the real world. There you could become a superstar or a slave, even a man or a woman. I never knew who or what I was going to be until I sat down and started to write. I love the fact that as long as I was writing the story, no one else's opinion really mattered. I was in control of my own world. There is no one that could tell you what to do in that world but yourself. I had been doing this for my whole life. It was how I made sense of the world that we live in.

When I am writing, I can become anybody or anything. I wrote all types of books, from love stories to slasher books. The more blood the better is what my son would say. I was just a big nobody, and until I accepted that, I just had a lot of stories bouncing around in my mind. Then one day I put an idea on paper. That was that; I was hooked! I knew that my writing was how I could go anywhere and be anybody. It set me free, you could say. My mother told me not to listen to what people said about me but to give them something to talk about. That way, they could say what they wanted to say, but if they told the truth, you are the one in control and happy.

Printed in the United States
By Bookmasters